the square donut

a novel by

lauren crane

ISBN 978-0-9987287-0-4

www.thesquaredonut.com

Published and printed in the U.S.A.

Library of Congress Control Number: 2017905467
Backyard Bird Publishing, Pleasant Ridge, MI

The Square Donut/Lauren Crane, First edition—May, 2017

Jacket Design and Artwork: Sarah Sarwar
Editing: Lisa Cerasoli and Adrian Muraro
Interior Design: Danielle Canfield

This book is written with gratitude for life, love and the beauty to be found in nature—human and otherwise.

the
square
donut

So, Anyway

I hate this town. It's all bunched up, limp and sour, like a dishrag. Dishrag, Ohio, that's where I live. Now, I've got nothing personal against dishrags. I just hate everything.

Oh, yeah, I'm Toby. Toby Renfrew, future heiress reluctant to The Precinct Donut Emporium: Home of the square donut with the amazing pink icing. My dad came up with the slogan because he's a regular donut laureate. Hey, I've got nothing personal against my dad; he's just teetering with the rest of this town, on the brink of the great stink-lake Erie.

Now, you probably think I'm down about everything, and maybe I am. What can I say? I'm nothing if I'm not honest, and believe me, I'm nothing. I'm a blank wall staring at a blank wall. I'd say my life is vanilla, but vanilla is a flavor. My life has no flavor, just like the pink icing.

I've got to make some changes.

. . . . .

A girl was in our shop the other day. I didn't think she was from around here, so I wasn't obligated to hate her.

Funny how she just suddenly appeared; I turned around and there she was, sitting on the stool I'd just finished duct taping. My dad calls it duck tape. Quack.

So, anyway, this chick came in and ordered a jelly-filled and some coffee and pulled out a cigarette. She was about my age—seventeen, I guess—and giving me the eye, I think. Then I wondered what I was thinking.

"Got a light?" she asked.

I was bored, I had a book of matches, so I struck one and held it up. She leaned forward and started puffing, not taking her eyes off mine. I poured her coffee real slow.

"Sugar?" I asked.

"Yes, dear?" she asked.

"I mean, um, do you want sugar?" I fumbled.

"Um, yes dear," she said.

I grabbed the dispenser from down the counter and before I could put it in front of her, she pointed to her cup, indicating that I should pour it in. Being in the service industry, I of course obliged.

Before the sugar could reach her cup, she put her hand out to catch it. I jerked to a stop. She licked the sweet stuff from her palm, eyes still on mine. My heart was playing a conga. As she tipped her hand for more, my eyes lingered on her wrist. I saw a botched suicide stitched across the soft part. She saw me see. I winced out a fake smile; she stared. I pretended someone else needed coffee.

For a brief moment, I sensed a taste of something. Then nothing, except maybe a decent tip.

. . . . .

My dad opened the shop when he was single. (My so-called "mother" joined him sometime later.) My dad wanted to be a cop, but didn't meet the height requirement. My guess is he thought the next best thing, short of being a cop, was to hang with cops, so he opened The Precinct Donut Emporium. My brother, Friday, was the firstborn. I showed up next, circa 1960, sliding headfirst into a world of grease, bad coffee, and abandonment—my mom ran off with the sugar supplier when I was two. She came around once after that, I heard. I was about six, I think. We weren't introduced. I don't know if she's still with the sugar guy or not with the sugar guy, because everyone's hush-hush on the subject. That's okay. I really don't care. Much.

My mother was an orphan, so they say, no relatives to speak of—and like I said, no one does. My dad obliterated any and all photos, which means I don't even have a picture of her other than the one in my head. I see her as being a lot like that actress Suzanne Pleshette. I have tried to hate my mother, but who can hate a woman who looks and talks like that?

My dad's still bitter. And paranoid. We buy our sugar at the Pick 'n Pay.

. . . . .

We've lived above the shop always, my dad and Fry and me, in a skinny, two-story brick building that's ancient, creaky, old. In the winter, the furnace belches and the radiators hiss. It gets pretty cold here by the lake, and those radiators get hot. (Understatement.) Friday and I used to have contests over who could keep their feet on the radiator the longest. (His brainy idea.) It kind of hurt, so I'm not sure if the winner was actually a winner.

My dad got a bargain on the rundown place way back when, about 1950, I guess, and rolled up his sleeves to turn his donut vision into reality. He got his hands on the remains of some out-of-business 1930s soda shop and installed this relic of a wood counter. He put a black

4

and white speckled linoleum top on it and screwed a dozen chrome stools into the wood floor in front. Half of the stools have the original black leather on the seat, four have made the switch to black and white checkered vinyl, and two are in the duct (duck!) tape transition stage.

On the Employees Only side of the counter, where yours truly has wasted her youth, is the stainless-steel BUNN-O-Matic Coffee Maker that's always pumping out the brew. Next to that is three tiers of wood shelving speckled with the day's donuts.

Dozens of people come through our door every day. Some just pick up their donuts and leave, saying things like, "I shouldn't, but once in a while can't hurt, ha, ha," and then twenty-four or forty-eight hours later they're in again saying, "I shouldn't, but once in a while can't hurt, ha, ha." Others sit in the booths or at the counter, eating donuts, drinking coffee, and discussing their personal matters, someone else's personal matters, how business is down, how prices are up, how the weather's too hot, how their spouse is too cold, how the fish are biting, how the government stinks, how the fishing stinks, how the government bites, how their roof toilet hot water heater basement pipes leak, baseball, football, balls of all kinds, liars and cheaters and lovers, oh my. I give some conversations a two-cup rating, some a four; others I know in advance to put on a second pot.

Nearly thirty years of donuts have been baked into the walls here. Seventeen years' worth baked directly into my skin. I know it's true because once, some little kid bit me. When asked why, he said, "Her 'mell like a cookie."

That's me, a five-foot-five, dishwater blonde, brown-eyed cookie.

Oh, yeah, and I'm "solid." One of our regulars, Miss Helen, who is like sixty or a hundred years old, always hugs me and says, "You're so solid!" Which, to me, is a code word for "fat." She used to drive me nuts. I've noticed that Miss Helen is looking solid herself these days.

I am defined by our customers: "Can I get a refill, kid honey sweetie dear blondie young man—oh, I'm sorry, young lady?"

"Aren't you a big little grown up immature smart smart-alecky sweet chubby cute tomboy?" Sometimes it's hard for me to know where the shop ends and I begin.

When my dad started his great donut adventure, he hired his old friend, Kasper, from the bakery in Cleveland—where they both worked when they were kids—as The Precinct's head donut-maker. The big donut-head, that's what Friday calls him. Well, not to his face. Kasper, who is thin, wispy, fair-skinned, and as tall as my dad is short, came from Poland when he was ten, and still has a little accent. He's a champion metaphor-mixer.

For instance, one of Kasper's buddies came in when Kasper was at the fryer and couldn't talk. Kasper gave him a friendly wave and said, "Okay, we'll get together and chew the shit later, then." Or if someone's self-sabotaging, he regularly utters: "I tell you, that guy's just shooting himself in the balls." Friday loves it when Kasper butchers a phrase. He lives for it.

Min is our waitress in charge. She takes the title seriously, because she sure acts like she's in charge, which is another way of saying she's bossy, but I don't mind. Min is Olive Oyl skinny with a Jiffy Pop pooch of a stomach. I think she wears padded bras, because her boobs cave in a little when she wears a t-shirt, like when we go on our annual Precinct outing to watch the Cleveland Indians play. She mostly wears a waitress uniform, though—her choice, she says because it makes her "feel like a professional."

Here's Min in action: Let's say it's a Tuesday morning and a couple—we'll call them Fred and Eloise—walk in at seven-thirty. (Their names are likely to be Fred and Eloise, since Fred and Eloise walk in here every Tuesday morning at seven-thirty.) Fred and Eloise are in their forties or fifties. I don't know exactly; I just know they're really old and they've been coming here since before I was born.

So, let's say it's a Tuesday morning, and Fred and Eloise walk in the door. Min grabs a coffee pot and has their cups filled before they sit down, and yells, "Hey, Kid, a vanilla crème, a nutty cake, and an original square." Since it's seven-thirty on Tuesday, I already have the donuts on the plates. Min flies over like she's wearing a cape, swoops the plates off the counter, winks, and says, "Way to go, Kid."

That's when I hear Min say to Fred and Eloise, "When are you two lovebirds going to build a nest together?" And I hear Eloise say, "Oh, Fred and I are just friends, Min." And Fred says, "Intimate friends."

Eloise giggles and says, "Oh, Fred." Which I am mouthing because I've heard that conversation three hundred and twenty-seven million times. And now I get to memorize more conversations from open till close, since high school is over for good. (I was supposed to be in the "We Are Great Class of '78," but had the credits to graduate with the "Best from Hell to Heaven Class of '77." It seemed like a good idea at the time.) I talked to Friday about giving out conversation redundancy awards, but he said it would be bad for business, especially since I wanted to call them the "If-I-hear-your-story-one-more-time-I'm-going-to-barf Awards." I think Friday lacks an entrepreneurial spirit.

Friday, Friday, Fry. Three years older. A million years smarter. He's good as brothers go, always protecting me—though if you ask me, he always needed protecting more than I did. He's not all that tough. Except for this one day.

My friend, Pauline Green, and I were sitting on a bench in front of Wally's Roller World, eating a Kreamy Thing custard cone. (Wally's Roller World is two doors down from our shop, and The Kreamy Thing is on the other side of Wally's. The fun never stops in Dishragville.) Well anyway, these boys came out of Wally's, and one of them said to me, "Hey, you wanna ball me?" Now, I just thought it was a scream, what he said. Unfortunately for the kid, Friday was walking out of Wally's behind him, and he didn't think it was one bit funny. The kid ended up running away with a bloody nose.

My dad reprimanded Friday, but you could tell he was proud of him, too, defending my honor and all. As I said, I just thought the kid was funny. Around here, I need all the funny I can get.

But what was really funny—and I mean weird funny—was that Friday is not the bang someone in the nose kind of guy. He's a gentle soul. A perpetual turn-the-other cheeker. As I said, he's the nicest guy. Just don't mess with the people he loves.

· · · · ·

I saw that girl again. That girl. The one who wasn't from around here. Again, she walked into the shop without me noticing and sat on that stool. Only this time, she ordered a chocolate crème. I liked her looks. She had a Gracie Slick thing going—dark hair, ice blue eyes, and a cool intensity. She was wearing frayed jeans that dragged on the ground and bagged in the butt. I noticed her butt. Then I noticed I noticed her butt. I decided to brave the situation and talk to her. I was right, she wasn't from around here. She said she'd just been hitchhiking around for the summer. I envied that.

She was camping out at the old beach. Her name is Carolina.

Carolina. It's a really good name for a dark-haired, blue-eyed, skinny, suicidal hitchhiker I can't get out of my mind.

. . . . .

The Precinct Donut Emporium is across the street from the entrance of the old Lake Erie Beach Park that's been closed for a few years. The old beach was huge, but Lake Erie devoured it. Now, all that's left is a boarded-up beach house overlooking a scrawny strip of sand. But back in the sixties, when we were kids, it was a *beach*. There was a playground built right on it. We'd jump off the swings and land in the burning sand or rub waxed paper on the slide to see how fast we could go. There were times when old Erie would crawl right up to the equipment so that we could slide directly into the water. That was a blast.

At the height of Erie's pollution, when we couldn't go in, we'd spend the day counting dead fish.

The beach house is made of good lake rock. A massive stone porch runs around all four sides. Way back when, giant-sized screens covered the windows. Wooden screen doors squeaked open and banged shut. Popsicle-painted kids hung from the porch swings that dangled from the ceiling, while their mothers rocked, gossiped, and smoked. Inside, big brown ceiling fans mixed the air into one giant whiff of popcorn, hotdogs, Coppertone, and wet bathing suits. The concrete floor was always cold and forever covered with wet, sandy footprints.

Right in the middle of the place was a circular glass case filled with the best stuff in the whole world: balsa wood airplanes with rubber-band-powered propellers, beach balls, inner tubes, Frisbees, and pinwheels with little silver bells in the center. There were Slow Pokes, Red Hots, Pixie Sticks, and Sweet Tarts, candy necklaces, snow cones, and pop, and ice cream. It was a gourmet's paradise. Fry and I used to dine there regularly.

They padlocked the beach house after the beach disappeared. I learned how to jimmy the lock a while ago, and sometimes sneak in to sit on a silhouette of a park bench. There, I conjure up a movie in my head. A woman walks through the door. She's holding the hand of a toddler—a little girl. Both are wearing red and yellow polka dot bathing suits. The woman lets go of the toddler's hand to light a cigarette. As she's shaking out the match, the toddler reaches up and the hot match sears her hand. The toddler screams. I touch the tiny scar on my palm. I get a knife-sharp pain that rips from my belly to my throat. The pain never stops me from playing the movie. At least the pain is something.

The old beach is my place, the only part of living here I like, really. It's rundown and deserted. I can relate to that. When I go there, it's just me, the shadows and the light, the water or ice and snow, the rocks and sand of what little beach is left, corroded beer cans and my own rusty thoughts.

t w o

Missing in Action

Okay, I told you about how my mom split when I was two, which means my life has been my dad and Friday and the donut shop mostly. But it's been sprinkled with other people, too, like my dad's brother, Uncle Nick, his wife, Auntie Flo and her son, my cousin Mitch; my dad's mom, my late Grandma Pearl, and her third husband, the slightly later Lefty Wright; Kasper and Min, of course; and my favorites—grandma's cousin Emily and her friend, Emaline. This is my family. My blood. My bleed.

Anyway, I grew up, more or less, running around between the donuts and the beach—when it was one—and this bunch I've identified as family. It's a miracle that

I turned out anywhere near normal when you think about it.

Take my Auntie Flo for instance; she's a nut for gold spray paint. If it doesn't move, she'll paint it gold. One day, she has green plastic ivy; the next time you visit, it's gold. Once, when I was a kid, I made her a picture out of macaroni and, beating her to the punch, painted it gold. Next time I went over, she had gold macaroni everywhere. She glued it on lamps and picture frames and Kleenex boxes and cigarette cases. She had taken macaroni art to a whole new level.

Well, anyway, whatever isn't gold you can bet is red crushed velvet. Gold and red crushed velvet. Oh, yeah, and mirrors—the ones with the little *gold* veins running through them. The woman's got her taste and she loves it, and you've got to love her for loving it, since it makes her so happy. She's someone you really want to see happy since her son, my cousin Mitch, is MIA in Vietnam and all. They put his name on bracelets for people to wear around so nobody forgets him. As if we could.

So, you'd give anything to see Auntie Flo happy, especially at the end of one of those nights she's downed a few Miller Highlifes. Now, it's against her religion to drink alcohol, but I don't think even her fiery God could possibly blame her for it, considering the Mitch situation.

If you're with her on those nights, you get to see the ritual.

"I think I'll have me just one of those champagne of bottled beers," she says.

You sit back as she pours that Miller Highlife into a glass—she's a lady—and shakes salt in it for some unknown-to-me reason. Then you watch it all unfold. After a few of those salty Millers, she starts leaking like a holey hose. Tears seem to come through her skin. She cries from a deep well that's never dry. Sometimes I like to be there so I can cry for Mitch, too. Sometimes you just got to.

The funny thing about Vietnam was that for a long time, I thought being in a war was normal. I saw it, the war, on TV every night. They were always showing guns going off and bombs dropping and guys being carried on stretchers and people ducking under chopper propellers, dust flying, and news announcers in camouflage yapping into microphones. Then they'd show commercials. It was like a soap opera or something. Snap on the TV, find out what happened today, x-number of guys dead, x-number of guys wounded, x-number of guys missing (a.k.a. MIA). They turned people into numbers that flashed on the screen, then try to sell you "a little dab will do you" Brylcreem or the year's best new something of the century, then remind you to tune in tomorrow, same time, same place, for the next episode of *The War in*

Vietnam. The war was on the tube. The bullets stayed behind the glass, neat and clean.

And somewhere behind that glass, amidst all that confusion, beneath the shouting you couldn't hear and dust that left no residue was my cousin. I'd look for him—a guy with zero facial hair, a cheesy grin, and feet so big that he and everybody else tripped over them. I'd sit real close to the set to see if I could see him. I thought I did a couple times.

Friday didn't go to war; he just missed it. He said he wanted to go and find Mitch, but truthfully, I think Fry was just as glad he didn't have to. He gets heat rash, and he likes his legs.

My Uncle Nick, like I told you, is married to my Auntie Flo. He's a mailman, and Auntie Flo keeps his uniform all starched and crisp. When it's the day she irons the clothes, she props up her Holy Bible and goes at it. The more she reads (her preference leans toward fire and brimstone), the stiffer my uncle's shirts get. I hear she used to iron his boxer shorts, but that didn't last long.

Anyway, my uncle's a quiet man, a walking hush. He doesn't say much of anything to anybody. After he delivers the mail, he goes to The Tavern. He's not the religious kind, so his beer goes down with no excuse. Mitch wasn't his kid, but my Uncle Nick raised him, and you can tell he's pretty worried about him. Like my dad,

Uncle Nick's small, but he's also muscular, so it's not the mailbag dragging that postman's shoulders down.

I can't imagine what'd it be like taking a kid all the way through high school graduation—you know, all the birthday cakes and bikes and Band-Aids and braces, and all those times teaching him how to catch a baseball and buying him pimple cream and telling him about sex and girls and all that stuff—only to have him become MIA. And you kind of have no choice but to go crazy thinking about him all sad and hurt and lonely, and maybe bleeding or swollen up with infections, or hot with fevers, or bitten up by weird bugs or rats or maybe snakes, on the other side of the globe, in a jungle, probably being starved and beaten and tortured. It could haunt you and haunt you, and all you want to do is get him home and pour him some cold milk and make him your best cream puffs—because they were his favorite. And you remember him smiling with those braces on and remember how he looked the night he went to the prom, all handsome in that powder-blue tux, and he was always nice to everybody and made you feel special, and you hope he's okay and you pray he's okay, but you know he's not and you can't do one goddamned thing about it.

Yeah, sometimes the world is truly ugly. No wonder my aunt wants to paint it.

. . . . .

Mitch left in the fall of 1970. A couple days before he packed his duffle for good, he picked me up from school in his brand-new, slightly used, 1967 Deepwater Blue Camaro Convertible. I know the color because he gave me his car catalog to hold onto while he was gone, and the paint color was circled in red about twenty times. It was funny to me, the name Deepwater Blue. In Erie, the water is deep, but rarely blue. It might be called a Drainpipe Grey or a Wipe-your-nose-would-ya Green. But Deepwater Blue? Uh, no.

"Keep this for me, will you, Toby?" he said, handing me the catalog. "I don't want it to get lost in the shuffle at home." I caught his drift. My Auntie Flo was quite the collector of things, so there was a lot to shuffle over there. "And one more thing," he said. "And this is important."

It was so important that he had to pull over to tell me. We were taking the scenic route home, so he steered the car onto a clifftop overlook, where we could see the lake stretched out in all its grey-greenness below. He parked and turned off the ignition. The top was down on the Camaro (my request) and the breeze coming off the lake was misbehaving, twisting at my hair and making my nose run. It probably wasn't convertible weather. I'll never forget the smell of that day, though. Whenever I catch a whiff of the lake mixed with dead leaves, I think of me and Mitch parked up on that cliff.

"Slide over here," he said, getting out of the car and closing the door.

I slid over to the driver's seat.

"I'm going to teach you how to start this baby."

"Really?" I asked. "Cool."

"Yeah, and then once a week, you've got to go to my house and start her up. Otherwise, the engine will be dead when I get back."

"Cool, yeah."

He then gave me about a twenty-minute lesson on how to start the car. We're talking about a manual transmission and a fifth-grade girl, but I caught on and learned to do it. I don't know now if he was a great teacher or I was just the most willing kid on earth. I'd do anything for my cousin Mitch.

"I'm going to hang my keys right by the kitchen door of our house. Now, when you come over, make sure you're a little hungry, because my mom will be looking for somebody to feed."

So, every week after that, I began walking the two blocks to Mitch's house to start that Camaro, and my Auntie Flo would say that Uncle Nick had just started it that morning, or Friday had been around to start it (looks as if Mitch gave him the same lesson). But I'd go start it anyway. Then I'd end up sitting with Auntie Flo, watching one of her TV shows. Visiting. Eating her potpies.

Of course, now I know what my cousin was up to with the car-starting thing.

. . . . .

Mitch might have had a clever plan for the home front, but I don't think he knew what he was getting into over in Vietnam. He was always poetic and romantic when he talked about being a soldier. He wanted to be a Green Beret more than anything in the world. He couldn't wait to enlist—he was not going to wait to be drafted, not that boy. He had set up an obstacle course in the woods, chin-up bars, climbing walls, and hurdles made of tree branches along a narrow path. He and a buddy built it and timed each other. Mitch was trained and ready.

The Green Berets weren't ready for Mitch, though. He had to settle for being a regular soldier, but he was good with it. I didn't know the difference. He looked great in his uniform. I carry a picture of him all uniformed up in my wallet.

Yeah, in all of Mitch's grand schemes, I don't think coming up missing or dying played a part in his plan. Dying: that was a word no one spoke. But I guarantee we all thought it.

I'm thinking that dying was not part of that Carolina girl's plans, either. I'm thinking that gash of a scar across her wrist was her deciding to die, but she must have changed her mind, because she's here now. At least, I think she's still here. She's been MIA herself for four days.

Not that I'm counting.

three

It Was Trying to Rain

I cleaned and closed The Precinct. My dad likes every corner of the place to be militarily clean. Spit-shined down to the last spoon, which is a fairly gross thought. He's a very weird man. Not that clean is weird; he's just twisted in so many ways. A human cruller, you might say, if you knew your donuts.

It was trying to rain. I crossed the street to the old beach, passed the Closed to the Public warning sign, and squeezed through the hole in the fence behind the No Trespassing, This Means You! sign. I noticed that the letters were so faded I could hardly read them. I made a mental note to tell Zeke, the DPS guy.

I scanned the horizon, but didn't see her. I hadn't told myself that I was looking for her until I realized, again, my disappointment at not seeing her. It started to drizzle. I sat on my favorite rock and closed my eyes, holding my face up toward the mist and the sun streaking through the clouds. When I opened my eyes, she'd again performed her appearing act. There she was, at my feet, a silhouette against the Jesus rays.

"Gee-zus." She made me jump, and there was a thrill in it. "How do you do that?" I asked over my palpitations.

She gave me no answer.

Carolina sat down in front of me cross-legged, with one Earth Shoe-shod foot over the other. She looked me in the eyes and said, "I feel clean when it rains."

She is so deep. I wish I were. I wish I could have said something from my vulnerable, honest soul that would have held a simple yet brilliant universal truth.

"Well, you look pretty clean, I mean, after hitchhiking all over and camping and everything." I winced at the stupidity of my response.

She was silent.

I stumbled on. "I mean, you look like you shower regularly." I faded, miserably.

Carolina put her chin on her knees as she hugged them to her chest. Carolina rocked herself. Carolina smiled. The lake, the mist, the rays, and Carolina there in all her Grace Slickiness—what was a girl to do? All I could do was look at her. I blushed and felt something I can only describe as really good. And I felt really good down to the very deepest depths of my very blushed being.

It began to rain. Suddenly, I felt clean.

. . . . .

Carolina had set down stakes and was living in a pup tent at the old beach. She hid it in some of the scruff and trees by the water's edge. Somehow, she knew she had to hide. Maybe the No Trespassing sign was a clue, or maybe she saw Officer Wheedle, the local fuzz who was always looking for trouble, cruising the place. Or maybe she was just a girl who hid.

I started seeing her more after her Erie appearance. She'd materialize at odd moments, and we'd go out to get a burger at Steer's Beef 'n Chips, or go to the Erie Drive-In to catch *Saturday Night Fever* for the 1.4 millionth time. "Too bad they don't run *Eraserhead* here," she'd say. "You'd love it." Or we'd peruse Records! record store. "Let's go say hi to David." She'd look at every Bowie record every time.

Once, Carolina said, "Toby, your main street is Erie and your lake is Erie. A lot of things here are Erie."

"Yeah," I said. "Erie, as in eerie, weird, rancid, old, stinky."

She paused, looking around. "I like cruddy. It's cruddy, in a cool way."

Cool? That was a new and unexpected point-of-view.

I looked at the faded entrance arch to the old beach and our raggedy building. Across from us were the woods where Mitch had built his obstacle course. Next to us is The Tavern, which looks as if it were made of matchsticks. And who calls a bar a tavern anymore anyway? Next to that, Wally's Roller World, which I mentioned, where everything from the building to the rollers on the skates are worn and a little bit grubby. The Kreamy Thing, next to Wally's—as I also told you—was built during the Great Depression, which also describes its appearance, although the custard's pretty good. Cross the side street and you come to a yellow cinderblock motel called 40 Winks, where people used to bring the kids for a weekend by the lake. And where all the friends of the owner's kid, Bucky Salida, used to bring their high school dates. (Unbeknownst to Mr. and Mrs. Salida.)

Keep walking and you get to a few rental cottages that have seen better days, Harold's Auto Parts (complete with a picture window full of found-on-the-road hubcaps), and, sticking out like a beer belly in an all-white dress shirt, the Christ Almighty Baptist Church.

You've got more woods for about a quarter mile, then city hall, the fire station, and the police station. A snappy new and tacky subdivision full of cheap split-levels ends where the big intersection begins. There you'll find the Texaco, the Pick 'n Pay, the Dye Baby Dye hair salon (Min's second home), a bunch of stores too boring to mention, and the most beautiful place in the entire universe—Mandelo's Harley Davidson, a place, I discovered, where Carolina and I stand on common ground.

Unfortunately, I had to stumble over some uncomfortable territory to find it.

Up to the point when Carolina showed up, I'd always been good at thinking. After, um, not so good. I got a little busy looking at her, staring at her mouth (lips). It's kind of embarrassing, really.

What happens to me when I see Carolina—she scares me, she excites me, she intrigues me. The way she moves, like a baggie blowing in the wind real fast above the ground, hardly touching. And when she looks at me, she looks right through my eyes to my brain, right through my skin to my guts. I feel gut-naked in front of her. I've never met anybody like her in my entire life. She's my age, but a whole lot more worldly. I mean, she *hitchhikes*. She has my insides churning like a glass of Alka-Seltzer.

When she's not around and I get my brain back, questions surface. One keeps coming back. That scar on her wrist. What the hell?

I know everybody's got scars, because they like to talk about them. My dad's friends come into the shop and lift up their pant legs, (or worse, open their shirts).

"Shrapnel, Dubya Dubya Two."

"Enemy fire, Korea."

"Unfortunate mishap, John Deere."

Kasper said he knew a guy who had "his whole leg decapitated."

I wanted to know about Carolina's scar. Attempted suicide? Why?

So one day when we're wading in the waves of Erie, I mention it, kinda casual.

"Um, so, what's with the scar on your wrist?"

"Smooth entrée," she said.

"Just wondering."

"Uh-huh."

There was silence for a while, during which I was internally wigging out, sure I blew everything. Whatever everything was.

"It was an accident," she said.

"Oh good, a car accident?"

"Toby, car accidents aren't good, they're fabulous, what with the rolling heads, flying limbs and all."

"I didn't mean car accidents are good, I—"

"It was an accidental suicide attempt."

I likened her story to one I'd heard where some guy claimed he accidentally stabbed his wife seventeen times.

It didn't cut the cake, but I was getting that sick-to-my-stomach-wish-I-never-brought-it-up feeling and was really looking to wrap it up.

"Listen, Toby, life was shit, complete shit, and I wanted out. So I took a swipe with a razor, only I changed my mind, which is a little tricky once you slice a vein. I don't recommend it to anybody. People get all hot about it, and the next thing you know you're in the mental ward of a hospital wishing you had succeeded, and the only thing that keeps you going is the thing you wanted to live for in the first place."

"Which is what?" I asked.

"A Harley. I thought riding a Harley would be better than dying. Plus, it would get me away from my life."

"I love motorcycles."

"You'd be crazy not to."

We both jumped on the motorcycle topic, and redlined it until we were miles away from the suicide subject. Even so, the suicide thing, the Mitch thing, the death thing, burns my brain. I don't get it.

Let's say you make it through the rickets and get yourself old. You've got scars, sure. And you've seen a ton, unless you get there with your eyes closed, which I know some people do. (You meet a lot of characters in the donut business.) Just when you've got the fat part of life under your belt, you die. I don't mean to insult whoever's in charge here, but that's dumb. You just die?

Where does all that learning go? Into the ground? Into a pile of ashes? Into the mud in the Winner's Circle at Thistledown Racetrack, like my Grandma Pearl?

Like I said, my Grandma Pearl was married to Lefty Wright. Lefty was a horse trainer from way back. They raced the horses at Thistledown when the weather was good here. In the winter, they'd climb into an old converted school bus that was painted army green, horses and all. (Well, the horses weren't painted green; I'm just saying they—my grandparents—would actually get in the bus with the horses and head south to race.) Grandma Pearl and Grampa Lefty, well, they loved it when "their" horses won. They never owned the horses; only fat, rich guys did. Grampa Lefty was fat, in a Humpty Dumpty kind of way, plump in the middle with skinny little legs. But he wasn't rich, which kept him from owning horses, but not from loving them. So, when the horses Grampa Lefty loved won, man, the old folks got pee-your-pants excited. They'd stand there in the Winner's Circle, proud as proud, the rooster and his chicken. (He called her "My Chicken.") There was no place they'd rather be.

So when Grandma Pearl died, she was the first to leave, well, my dad, Uncle Nick, and Grampa Lefty decided the natural place for her to be was in The Winner's Circle at Thistledown.

It was raining the day we spread her ashes—those bits of Pearl, as I like to say. I imagined her getting stuck on a thoroughbred's foot and racing around the track. I was thinking about that while we were standing there. Friday elbowed me and told me to wipe the big grin off my face. I couldn't help it if I didn't feel like crying; it was a cool picture.

Two years later, we did the same with Lefty Wright, or as I like to pun: what was left of Wright. He flew around with the leaves and the dust. Some of him blew up on me and got caught in my hair, which meant it was highly likely that part of that big, cigar-chewing old man was washed down the drain with the Prell later that night.

And that gets me thinking....

Okay, so you're living and you're breathing and you're making all your choices. And blood is pumping through you, churning around, feeding all your parts, and you haul that body around with you, or I guess I'd say, your body hauls you around with it. Well, why not take chances and be great? You're just going to end up dried up or rotten or washed down some drain and g-o-n-e gone. Why don't you do something? Why don't I do something? While I've still got blood in me, why don't I do something? I feel stuck in a big fat vat of spoiled molasses. Sucked down. I can't move my arms.

Then I think of Carolina. I see her every day, those X-ray eyes, my seltzer stomach. When she floats into my sight, it's like I'm being slapped by the hand of February. She's cold wind in my lungs. She makes me breathe deeper, in sharp bursts. She makes me see clearer, though only glimpses. We take long barefoot walks along the lake. We talk and she'll make a comment, a smartass comment that I don't quite understand exactly, and I get a peep of something. I try to hold onto the sight, but it comes and goes quickly. I keep feeling like I'm on the verge of something huge. I'm Christopher Columbus; Isabella's kissed me off and I'm sailing toward the new shore. I think I see land, the lush green land, and then the sea goes flat. No New World in sight, just the square donuts with the amazing pink icing, which, I must tell you, are not one bit amazing to *me*. Oh, don't get me started.

Maybe I should tell you about Grandma Pearl's cousin, Emily, who shares her house with the sweetest old lady, Emaline. Cousin Emily and Cousin Emaline. Em & Em. That's what I call 'em. They say they've been together since nineteen-forever.

The Ems live in a big, old, yellow house with one of those attics you see in movies with every bit of junk you can imagine. I used to love playing there up in the hot, dry air, walking on those squeaky floors, sneezing the whole time from the dust. Once, I went nuts over an ancient typewriter, so they gave it to me. They put in a new ribbon and greased the thing up. They told me to type up my thoughts, things I wonder about. I do a lot of wondering while I'm making the donuts. I even wonder in my spare time. I wonder what this old typewriter knows. This was Emily's typewriter, and I know it means a lot to her. In her day, Emily was a newspaper reporter. In her day. What the heck does it mean? Do we all have a day? What if this is my day? Lord, I hope not. What if I never have my day? "In her day, ol' Miz Renfrew was quite the...was quite the...was...what the hell was she?"

I took Carolina to the Ems one day. We had a time, the four of us, hanging out. The Ems kept bringing out the food. Carolina eats a lot for a skinny girl. It was a Sunday. I had taken the day off—a rare treat, I might add, Sunday being a big day for donuts. Cousin Emaline asked me if I thought any more about going to college. As if I'd been thinking at all about going to college. How can I go to college if I don't even know what I want to do with my life? I only know what I know how to do. I know how to make donuts and coffee. I know how to fill sugar and creamers. I know how to mop counters. I know how to pay bills. I know how to post ledgers. I can do every part of this business. My dad can go fishing for days at a time. He can catch walleyes or whales or what-the-hell-ever and know everything will be all right when he comes back. I'm good. And I hate what I'm good at. But I don't know what else to do. Yeah, I'm stuck in, sucked in, socked in molasses. I'm suffocating. "1-Adam-12, 1-Adam-12: possible suffocation on Erie Street. Over."

We stayed with the cousins late into the night. Cousin Emily asked Carolina if she'd like to take a break from camping and stay with them for a while. Carolina said she'd think it over and let 'em know.

On the way back, in the car, she was real quiet, thinking it over, maybe. She makes my heart beat a little too fast. She said she loves the cousins. She asked if I'd like to camp out with her. We stopped at The Precinct (which feels to me like the county jail) to pick up my sleeping bag and tell the old man—which is sometimes what I refer to him as in my head when I'm feeling like I hate this town, which I do more and more every day— what my plans were. He was busy dreaming about the one that got away, so I just grabbed my bag and pillow and Carolina and I headed out for the old beach.

I threw my stuff next to hers in the tent and crawled in. She turned on a tiny battery-operated lamp. I unrolled my bag. She was lying on top of hers, head propped up on her hand, watching me. Silent. I looked over and giggled, kind of nervous.

"Move your bag closer," she said.

It was a very small tent. It was hard to get closer, but I obeyed. Once my bag was in place I laid down, a mirror to her, on my side, head in hand, and smiled.

"This is cool," I said. "I'm glad they haven't kicked you out of here."

"Why's that, Toby?" she asked.

I stumbled a bit. "Um, because, I, like, you."

"Yes," she said, "I think you do." Then she reached over and put her hand under my shirt, running her fingers from my waist up to the bottom of my bra and then down again. I looked into her face. It was soft, like it was lit by a candle instead of a battery-operated lamp.

I felt scared, but I did not want her to stop. No, I did not want her to stop. She looked me in the eyes. "Take this off," she said, tugging at my shirt.

I obliged.

Still staring into my eyes, as if reading me, she undid my bra. A soft sound blew through her lips.

"Oh, Toby, you are beautiful."

The word "beautiful" was like a sudden punch to my brain. Only once had anyone ever used a word like that to describe me. I felt dizzy for a minute. She moved closer and touched my nipple with her tongue. The moan that came from me surprised me. She took my breast into her mouth, so warm and wet. I pushed her away gently.

"Take your shirt off," I whispered.

She did. Suddenly I knew what beautiful meant.

She kissed me. We kissed. The night was filled with nothing but us. With tongues and touch and magic and a sense of attachment I never felt ever before. And I laughed and I cried. We were wet and awake and sleepy, wired and tired. I fell asleep, eventually, somewhere on a cloud.

I woke the next morning alone in that little pup tent of hers. I slipped my t-shirt on over my naked self and stepped out. It was early; the sun was barely there. I focused and vaguely made out a figure and walked to her. There she sat, the lake washing over her naked body. I jerked my head around to see if anyone else was seeing what I was seeing. No one else was around. She looked up at me and smiled in that way she does.

"Carolina, what are you doing?"

She reached for my hand and I let her take it. She pulled me down next to her. She looked at me sleepily and the waves moved up my legs. She kissed me. Words were whirling in my brain: *What if someone? Shouldn't. No, too naked.* I pulled away a little. "Carolina, you should put some clothes on."

Carolina put her hands on my shoulders and pushed me down on the sand. She pulled her non-clothed self on top of me, pinning me down, kissing me. I struggled, wanting between the worry. She kissed me harder, touching me gently. I lost my train of thought. A new train pulled in. Forget this town. Forget the donuts. Forget everybody. I hate this town. I'll leave this town. I'll never look back. Never look back. Never look back.

I drew her in. She looked me in the face and ran her finger along my cheek.

Then she jumped up and walked, nakedly, into the lake.

I sat up, confused, staring at her. She looked back, but I couldn't read the words on her face. I followed her into the water. If the lake had been the boiling lava of Hell, I still would have waded in.

As I got closer to her she disappeared under water, popping up farther away. I moved in her direction. She did it again.

"Carolina."

She did it again.

I felt tired. I didn't want to play. I just wanted her. She popped up again.

"Carolina."

She disappeared again.

"Carolina!"

She was nowhere to be seen. I thrashed through the water toward the last place I'd seen her. I looked around. No movement. No sound.

"Goddammit!"

I started crying. I stood there like a damned baby bawling my eyes out. I felt something bump my leg and Carolina popped up next to me, smiling. I kept crying. I didn't try to hide it. I didn't like her *dis*appearing act. I didn't like it one bit.

"What's wrong?"

I cried harder.

"What, Toby, what?"

I cried harder. She started crying.

Carolina's with crying like some people are with barfing. They see someone else throwing up and they have to heave, too. And me, well, I was just emotional. Now, it could have had something to do with what happened the night before. Between Carolina and me. I. Between us. Anyway, well, I never made love before. I mean I never had sex at all. With anybody. Hardly a kiss. And I knew how I'd been feeling about her, but we're girls and, well, I knew about the Ems, but I didn't know much of anything, really. And, well, as I said, I was feeling emotional.

So, I was crying and Carolina started crying. She put her bare-naked arms around me and held me close to her bare-naked heart. My heart wasn't feeling much too covered up itself. So there we stood, in that stinking lake, my lover and I, my lover and I, my lover and I, in the steamy dawn holding on, bits of dirt and lake gunk stuck to our skin, hair all matted down, bodies damp, tears falling, chests moving in and out, lungs grasping for air.

If I wasn't so young, I'd use the word "weary" here. I was weary and she was a human rest stop. The world was a screaming rock concert and she was the Cleveland

Public Library. She was the shush, the Dewey Decimal System. I now knew exactly where I belonged.

But of course, me, Miss Responsibility, eventually realized I had to go to work.

When I arrived, The Precinct was already open. I crept guiltily up the back steps to the apartment and took a shower. When I went back downstairs to the kitchen, my dad, characteristically quiet, nodded as I came in. I started a new pot of coffee. I felt as if there was a mist around me. Like the white fog of mosquito repellent they spray on summer nights.

four

Not a Good Idea

So, you could ask, "What are you, some kind of lesbo or something?" And I'd shrug my shoulders in a "Who knows?" kind of way. I didn't wake up and say, hey, I think I'll kiss some girl. I'm not going to explain too much. I can't, anyway. But I will tell you that I had been some kind of walking iceberg. I told you right off how I hate everybody in this town. It's a lot of work, but I do it. Sometimes when somebody does something really funny I laugh, and when I laugh I find myself liking them. But for the most part, my heart's been ice, my brain's been numb.

So imagine my surprise when I saw Carolina and I felt what I felt. When I felt like I never felt before. When I felt like I saw other people feel in the movies. Goofy and lightheaded and plop-plop fizz-fizz stomached. When a little voice inside me started yelling like the Wicked Witch, "I'm melting, I'm melting!" If I get any sweeter, I'm going to have to give myself insulin. If I get any more lightheaded, I'm going to float away.

"What are you, some kind of lesbo?" That was Friday's question. He had this giant grin as he walked into the front room where Carolina and I were watching TV. We were sitting on the couch; I had my arm around her shoulder. To tell the truth and nothing but, if I had heard him come in, I would have moved away.

"Hey, can't I have a friend?" In retrospect, I see that my response may have been a tad defensive.

"Well, Your Bitterness, that would be news," he said.

Just then, Carolina leaned over and planted a long one right on my lips. She smiled at me, then at Friday.

"Yikes," Friday said. Then he turned and left the room.

I was panicked. I'd been exposed. Exposed by the person I was roses-and-chocolates in love with, to the person I've shared well, everything with, my entire life. I suddenly felt like I was going to lose. And lose big.

"Well, he shouldn't ask the question if he doesn't want to know the answer," Carolina said.

I was quiet. He shouldn't ask the question if I don't want to know the answer, either.

No, I didn't say that out loud. You don't say a whole lot out loud here in pissy Dishrag, USA.

. . . . .

One day, though, I did get loud. Really loud for me.

I was mopping up the counter when I saw this big truck hauling two bulldozers pull up Erie and stop right across from our place. I wondered (out loud) what the heck was going on, and my dad proceeded to tell me in his quiet monotone way that the old man who owned the woods died and his family sold them to a developer who planned to build apartments.

First of all, I never knew an old man owned the woods. I'd never given it any thought. The woods were *The Woods* and they were just there, period. All us kids would play in them for endless hours. It was a very cool place. We'd play war, killing each other with sound effects and arguing about whether we were dead or not. We'd gone in there and caught pollywogs and frogs and snakes. There were two huge old trees that had been downed by one storm or another, or maybe they just got tired of standing; anyway, we tied a couple of ropes on the trees near those that had fallen. We used to climb up on the uprooted part, which had to be as high as one of those flimsy split-levels, and grab onto the ropes and jump. Lord, that was fun. We built forts. Snow forts in

43

the winter. There wasn't a season that was lost in those woods. So, no, I wasn't happy with the news of the unknown old man, those huge yellow bulldozers, or with my dad.

"Why didn't you tell me?" I demanded, as if he owed me.

My dad blinked, thinking. "Well, people've been talking about it. Where've you been, Bee?"

He's called me "Bee" since I can remember. Sometimes he calls me "Bum-blee-bee."

"I've been here, I didn't hear, why didn't you tell me, don't you know it matters to me—the woods. They can't bulldoze the woods, assholes. We've got to stop them, can't we stop them, go stop them!"

I was spewing all over the place.

"Bee. Calm down. There's nothing you can do," he said. Fortunately, he didn't catch the "assholes."

But I didn't calm down. "You going to just sit here and do nothing? Didn't anybody say anything? Apartments? *Apartments?* They can't do this."

"Bee. They can and they will. You just settle down now," he said, monotone drone in my ear. "And watch your language."

"Sorry, but I'm not going to just sit here and let them do this."

I threw down my dishrag and slammed through the door. I didn't know what I was going to do but I was damn well going to do it. Just to prove it, I paused to kick the gravel in the driveway out front before stomping across to the commotion. Zeke, the DPS guy was there, "stupidvising," as my dad would say.

"Zeke," I said.

"Hey, Toby."

"Don't let 'em do it."

"Ever seen a John Deere biggis at one ere, Toby?"

"Zeke, you jerk, don't let 'em tear down the woods."

Zeke spat tobacco and looked at me sideways, saying nothing. I think he was hurt by the jerk part. I was sorry I said it, but too angry to apologize.

I turned on the next guy, an official-looking one who wore a suit with his hard-hat. Nice look.

"Hey, you, what are you doing?" I said, shoving my finger at him, interrupting his conversation with the bulldozer guy.

He gave me a sour look.

"You can't do this," I said. Yeah, I was tough.

"We can and we are, little lady," the suit said as he waved me off like I was a gnat.

Not a good idea.

"Hey you bassssssstard, I'm talking to you." The reference to the circumstance of his birth came out like a 78 rpm record set on 45, low and slow. I slapped down his official-looking metal clipboard. I was so angry I shocked myself, but the woods had always been mine. I

45

was shaking, tears in my eyes, hands in tight fists. I was ready to Mohammed Ali him into bloody oblivion. He was about to be stung by the Bee. That's when Friday reached down, picked up the clipboard and dusted it off.

"Sorry, man, we grew up in these woods." He put his hand on my shoulder.

I dropped the big "F" right then. Felt like the occasion deserved it.

The suit said, "Behave yourself, little girl."

Walking back to The Precinct, I couldn't say anything to my brother. My dad was standing at the door watching. My guess was he'd sent Friday to retrieve me. I couldn't look at him. I went up the back steps to my room. "What the hell? What the hell?"

Carolina was still in bed, having basically moved in by this point. "Bastards, all of them," I said as I fell into the space she made for me.

The morning hadn't started out too good. It was a Sunday and I had woken up late. My dad does not like me being late to work, especially since it's just downstairs. Especially on Sunday mornings when half the population of Northeast Ohio wakes craving donuts and flocks and gaggles and herds and bevies of the fat- and sugar-starved bloat our little shop. I eventually joined the frenzy which lulled, finally, at about eleven o'clock.

My dad, Friday, and I were sitting at the counter recuperating over cups of coffee. I've never quite gotten used to the bitter taste of the stuff, but I've been hooked for life from an early age. Kasper and Min were in the back, where Kasper was gently lecturing Min about her new boyfriend, who seemed to have a great deal of "affluence" over her. Which, of course, made Friday giggle.

"Maybe he's rich," I said.

Which made Friday snort. My dad changed the subject.

"I don't like the wandering around, sleeping outside, and hitch-hiking that this girlfriend of yours is doing."

I stopped mid-sip at the word "girlfriend."

Friday shot me a brotherly look—*now this should be interesting.*

"So, I talked to your Uncle Nick about the situation," my dad continued. "Nick said Flo didn't want to meddle. My thought was it might help them all, what with the rough state the two of them are in. But, no."

My cousin Mitch shot across my mind, pushing tears into ducts, just before my dad's words sunk in.

"You talked to Uncle Nick about Carolina?" I asked.

"It's not safe for the girl," he said, "and Officer Wheedle's been nosin'."

"Oh Lord, Dad, Wheedle's just a fat, stupid—"

His look stopped me from saying more.

"I think we just need to look out for the girl," he continued. "So, I was thinking, we've got the space upstairs, if you don't mind sharing your room."

Friday sputtered and spit his coffee. Everywhere.

"Son?" My dad looked puzzled.

"Nothing. Nothing. Nothing, nothing, nothing. I've got to uh do some...thing in the...." Friday pointed to the kitchen as he walked toward it.

"What do you think?" My dad turned, looking me square in the eyes.

I steadied myself. "Uh, um, sure, yeah. That'd be real nice. I'll ask her if she wants to. Sure."

He smiled, picked up his newspaper and tapped me on the head with it. "That's my girl," he said as he got up and joined the others in the back.

I felt as if Bob Eubanks from the *Newlywed Game* had just awarded me an entire studio full of prizes chosen 'specially just for me. I looked around for *Candid Camera* and signs of Allen Funt: "We've put a hidden camera behind the BUNN-O-Matic. Watch now as a father mischievously asks his seventeen-year-old daughter if she would mind sharing her bedroom with her lesbian lover."

There was no Funt and no Eubanks. All I saw was business as usual.

I looked at Friday. He had never made it to the kitchen.

He looked at me and shook his head in disbelief.

I took off my apron, yelled in the direction of the kitchen that'd I be right back, and I ran. See Toby run. See Toby jump. See Toby happy for once in her whole damned life. I ran myself to the old beach and threw myself into the sands of Carolina.

The Rolling Stone

I'm thinking about Vietnam. And I'm thinking how I bet the people who live there would love to live a life as mundane as mine. To understate the obvious: living in this mildewed town is better than living in the aftermath of having had your head shot at every day, or having had your hut burned, or your whole family mutilated. I venture the Vietnamese would rather have had their jungles plowed under for apartments than napalmed. Not that all that justifies the bulldozers or the Novocain-brained, shutter-eyed living that goes on around here. No. But sometimes, I like to grand-scheme things to see what makes sense.

I think about Mitch and Vietnam all the time. And then the grand-scheming starts. I jump to World War II and the Holocaust. I think it's kind of weirdo, psycho that I think about it so much. But I do. I've been this way ever since I read *The Diary of Anne Frank* in the eighth grade. She and her family spent years in a little attic hiding to save their lives. What was their crime? Oh, the Nazis had an answer for that question.

I had a lot of questions, too, so I kept reading about it. Maybe too much? I spend a lot of time trying to figure the whole thing out. I think about being taken away from everything that you've ever known, and having everything and everyone taken away from you, and there you are at the mercy of malicious, violent, so-called "people."

Biologically, yes, those Nazis were people. They lived their lives just like people. The Nazis had wives and kids and pets. In the evenings those Nazis gathered their loved ones around the dinner table—give papa a hug my little kinders honey pass the sauerkraut. They would spend their days pushing Jewish and Gypsy and Black moms and dads and kids, gay people, dwarfs, handicapped people (and anyone else who didn't fit the Nazi idea of the perfect German) into train cars with no food, no water and, um, no bathrooms. If it was subzero out, the people would freeze. Stifling hot, imagine it, shoulder to shoulder in the belly of a closed steel freight car. The destination for these travelers were the concentration camps, where they were stripped of clothing and any dignity they had left and sent in large groups to the "showers" to be gassed to death, or into the camps to be brutalized, starved or worked to death, or experimented on in torturous ways by real doctors before being killed—I will spare the details. Oh, and all these unwilling passengers were charged regular fare for their train tickets. (Although the children rode to their death for free.) They were just doing their job, these Nazis. Clock in, murder people, come home, tuck the kids into bed and on Tuesday nights play cards with the neighbors, who were somehow ok with the whole thing too.

Right about now, my dad would be telling me I'm taking wild leaps in logic, but since he's not me, I will just get this out of my head.

Old suit and hardhat ripping down the woods seems to me the same kind of character as those rifle-toting German soldiers. No, trees aren't people, but they are living things just going about their business. Standing tall. Beautiful. And purposeful. And hardhat, seemingly without a second thought, like those Nazis, *was just doing his job*. No conscience. Pulling life out by its roots. Killing. What are trees to him? A paycheck? You can't rebuild a 150-year-old thicket of trees. You can't bring back millions of murdered people. No. Gone. And someday we will be gone too. What will we have left behind? Sorrow. Mass graves. Cardboard apartments. I am like the Nazi neighbors. I should have chained myself to that bulldozer and defended those trees. But, instead, I make donuts.

. . . . .

I'm thinking about all this while mixing chocolate cake donuts. I have to be careful when I go on raging think fits. Too much handling (or angry stabbing) can make the donuts tough.

When I make donuts, I like to make the chocolate ones. They are donuts of substance. Flour, sugar, butter, milk, eggs, shortening, baking powder, baking soda, salt, vanilla, and unsweetened chocolate. I don't even measure any more. I can make them with my eyes closed. I make the dough, then cool it in the fridge. Cooler dough is easier to handle; you don't want to roll it too many times, that's another way you'll get a tough donut. Can't let that happen. I know they're only donuts, and I hate the fact that my life is donuts, but since I'm making them, they've got to be right.

Most of the time, I only make the cake donuts, plain, and chocolate. The Donut Head—I mean, Kasper—comes in way early and makes the main stash. My dad's in there, too. So's Friday. They all get into the dough. I come in mostly to serve it all up. Me and Min.

Min, like I mentioned before, has been here since forever. She's around my dad's age, give or take. Her hair color changes at unpredictable rates. Once, I swear, she went from blonde to brunette on her break. It's kind of fun to watch. Yep, that's what we do for amusement here in Rancid City.

Min, whose hair is currently what her hairdresser poetically proclaims to be "Luscious Licorice," has this fake crabby thing going. She's taught me the subtleties of crabby, although my crabbiness has a genuine quality. She says, "Keep'em guessin' where you're comin' from, Kid." She's always called me "Kid." I can talk to her easily. She gives me other advice, too. Like, "Always be the worst of two evils, it cuts down on the riffraff." Of which she's had her share, having been married and divorced four times. Or six? Who knows? One gave her a black eye. Once. That was her two-day romance/three-day marriage. She sent him to jail, then sent him packing. There were a lot of low-voice conversations at the time. I caught onto those early. Hanging with adults, I learned how to look like I wasn't listening while taking in every word. Sneaky, but highly educational.

Anyway, Min's got a lot of exes, and she's always on the lookout for ex-next. She was forever trying to get me to date some boy or another; the ones she picked special for me—well, the only requirement seemed to be gender. IQ, grasp of the English language, and daily hygiene habits did not seem to be of concern to her. She'd say men are good for one thing and one thing only, then wink at me, as if I had a clue what she was winking about. Well, I knew what she was referring to, but let's just say I was on a different wavelength. Lately, I am relieved to say, Min hasn't said much to me about "young studs." But she likes Carolina, I can tell. She calls her "Honey." Honey and Kid, that's us to her.

The Precinct doors are open from five forty-five a.m. until three every day. Sometimes, the three of us just sit and girl-talk a while after we close. Once in a while, Anna, Friday's gorgeous Amazon love, joins us. Anna has thick, white-blonde hair that hangs and moves like fabric. She stretches five feet eleven, and though not heavy, she's "oak solid," according to Miss Helen. "A big-boned girl," Auntie Flo says. A true Scandinavian, she wears snowflake sweaters in the winter, which makes her look like she just stepped out of a ski brochure. She's funny as hell, though less so lately.

The four of us were just sitting around one rainy afternoon when Min asked Carolina where she was from. Now, when I ask that question, Carolina just says, "From all over." And when I ask, "All over where?" she just smiles and changes the subject. So, on this day when Min asked her the question, Carolina sat back, lit a cigarette, shook the flame off the match, and said, "From Detroit, mostly."

Detroit's not "all over." It's just, over there. One lousy state away.

"What brings you to us, Honey?" Min asked.

Carolina exhaled smoke and said, "My thumb. I like to hitch. I got most of the way here on the back of a chopper, here from Pittsburgh. That's the last place I was. Before that, New York—the city, then the state. The city, that's a blast, but a drag, too. It's hard to breathe there. I like it here. It's all wide-open here."

She smiled at me.

I frowned a little. Disappointed, though I didn't know why.

She went on. "I've been hitchhiking around for two years, give or take. I've been a lot of places, met a lot of people."

"Huh," Anna said, a concerned look on her face. "Is your family still in Detroit?"

"Family's kind of a relative term," Carolina answered, then laughed a little, probably at the pun. "I suppose they're still there, still kicking. Inbreeding makes a hardy bunch." Then she laughed again, high-pitched, as she crushed out her cigarette and blew smoke out of the side of her mouth. "But really, I don't know and I don't care."

I was quiet, just listening. Watching. Inbreeding? I hope that was a joke.

Min took Carolina's chin in her hand and said, "Well, you've got family here, Honey, you just stick around a while."

Anna tucked a thick blonde swatch of silk behind her ear and smiled weakly.

Carolina got a funny look on her face and said she never really stays in one place too long because a rolling stone gathers no crap. She didn't look at me when she said it. Min did. I bit my lip. Min gave Carolina a pat on the hand and stood up.

"Well, I've gotta go. Got a date with Mr. Could-be-lucky-number-seven tonight."

That answered my how many husbands question. I wondered if he was the guy with affluence over her.

I walked Min to the door, feeling miserable for some unclear to me reason.

Min looked sympathetic and gave me a giant-sized kiss on the forehead. "I love you, Kid."

Anna slipped out behind Min after giving Carolina and me each a big hug. I was hoping for something funny here—I needed the comedic Anna, but she didn't appear.

I locked the door after them and turned the Open sign to Closed. I paused, thinking about what I wanted to say to Carolina. I suddenly had questions about who did what to my girl and why she was running. When I turned, I almost tripped over her.

"Whoa," I said.

"Whoa," she said back. "Whoa."

She started kissing me. She kissed the pout right off my lips. She kissed me toward the counter and pulled me down between the dirty dish sink and the order up window. My tongue grew numb as hers touched mine; the conversation it was poised to articulate never had a chance.

seven

Tru Lov

When we were at Erie High, Friday in the twelfth and me in the ninth grade, I got an eyeful of him in the hallway. The back of him, anyway—his front was busy being pressed up against some tall blonde babe, making out like nobody's business, only it was everybody's business right there in the not-just-any-hallway, but the hallway outside the cafeteria. During lunch.

As if high school wasn't miserable enough.

That was my first clue that he was dating someone.

Girls liked Friday a lot. They thought he was cute, which made me laugh out loud, but he wasn't so good at picking up their drift, even if it was of blizzard proportions. Mary Sharon Allison, also known as Mary Three-Names, would practically weep when she saw him. She was forever dropping pencils, notebooks, or whatever hint she had in her hand, hoping he'd stop and talk to her. He did stop to pick up things, just never the hint.

But Friday is the kind of guy who knows what he wants when he sees it, and he wanted the new girl from Minnesota—Anna Lovgren. Lovgren? Oh, my God, there were so many teases waiting for my brother in her name alone, but when I saw her face (finally, when it wasn't smashed against his) there were no teases in me. She's beautiful (as I may have mentioned before) with the biggest, whitest, widest smile and the reddest lips and, as I've said, she's funny. I've never seen my brother laugh so much in his life as when he's with Anna. Oh, and she's crazy smart.

The first time he brought her home for dinner, she smartly brought my dad an antique fishing lure. Reeled him in right away.

She brought me a leather journal.

"For your writing," she said. She is a flipping genius.

Friday is no science whiz, but he got the chemistry right on this one.

The phone rang in our apartment one night. It was Anna, but she wasn't calling for Friday. When he handed me the phone, his eyes flashed like the sun hitting Erie. I wondered what was up.

"Who is it?" I stage-whispered.

He just shrugged and walked away. I sensed from the back of his head that he was grinning. I knew the guy.

"Hello?" I said in the phone.

"Hi, Toby, it's Anna."

I had butterflies in my stomach. I felt like I had a celebrity on the line. If Stevie Nicks had been on the phone, I don't think I would have been more nervous.

"Oh, hi," I said.

"How are you?"

"Um, good. How are you doing?"

I was far more curious to find out the answer to, "Why are you calling?" but hung on patiently.

"I'm great. Hey, I was wondering if you'd like to go to lunch on Saturday, and maybe go shopping."

Lunch? Shopping? Me?

"Uh, sure," I said.

"Great! Is noon okay?" She was so enthusiastic I was beginning to believe it was great. Man, she was infectious.

"The donut shop doesn't close until three, so—" I couldn't finish my sentence, because Friday had suddenly reappeared and was rasping at me.

"Go, I'll cover for you, go."

"Oh, I guess noon is fine."

"Great!" she said again.

"Great!" I answered. "See you then." I hung up the phone.

"Isn't she great?" Friday was beside himself.

"Why would she want to have lunch with me?"

"She said she likes you and wants to get to know you," he said. "Isn't that great?"

Yeah, it was great, but what was I going to wear?

I ended up wearing my Levis and cowboy boots. I started out wearing my overalls and sneakers, but when I came downstairs, Friday said, "You're going like *that?*"

I didn't argue; I just turned around, went back upstairs, and changed.

"Okay?" I said, walking into The Precinct kitchen as my brother looked up from the sink full of dishes.

He didn't answer; he just stalked toward me, drying his hands.

"Do me a favor," he said, pulling out his wallet. "Buy Anna lunch."

"Sure, bro," I said. "Anything you say. Can I eat, too?"

"There's enough there," he said. "But here's another five if you need it."

There was definitely enough; Friday was generous to a fault. I pushed back his five. "Just kidding, man. Why are you so nervous?" (Why was I so nervous?)

"I just want you guys to have a good time, that's all."

I was about to reassure him that I already liked her, when his face became fluorescent, so I knew Anna had walked in the door. She was wearing gauchos with a gauzy blouse, an Annie Hall kind of vest, and a big smile that was all for Friday. I think he beamed himself over to her. No one could have possibly moved that fast.

After they kissed—a short one, for my benefit I'm sure—Anna and I left.

We drove to the mall in her mother's Mercury Cougar. It was a few years old, but still nice. She and her mom moved to Erie to live with her mom's sister while her dad was on some kind of Alaskan Pipeline security project. He was going to be gone for another year.

"Are you going to go to Alaska to visit your dad?" I asked.

"No, moose scare me," she answered.

I laughed.

Her face was dead serious.

"You're kidding, right?"

"No, Toby, I really have a fear of moose. It's an actual disease."

"A moose phobia?" I asked.

"Phobiamoositophia."

"Come on. Really?"

"It's serious, Toby," she said. "I have nightmares about moose. They wear little Elmer Fud hats and stalk me with hatchets. I can't even go into The Tavern because they have a moose head above the fireplace."

"That moose is very dead, Anna."

"It doesn't matter, Toby, it wasn't dead all its life."

I was trying to wrap my head around that statement, while at the same time re-piecing together my view of Anna.

"What about Bullwinkle?" I asked.

"Toby, Bullwinkle is a *cartoon.*"

"Right," I said. "Is it an antler thing?"

"No."

"Are you okay with reindeer?"

"I'm good with reindeer."

"Elk?"

"Fine."

"Captain Kangaroo—"

"Mr. Moose scared the shit out of me."

She found a parking space at the mall and pulled in just as I was concluding that my brother's girlfriend might have issues, but I was trying to be understanding. Sympathetic.

"I've heard about phobias. I watched this thing on TV about people who have a chicken phobia," I said. "It's called alek—"

"Oh God," she interrupted. "Who could be afraid of chickens? They make great pets."

Pets? I caught something on her face, but she changed it before I could identify the look.

We found a little restaurant in the mall, a dainty finger sandwich and tea kind of place. We sat down and looked at the menu. When the waitress came to take our order, Anna said, "Do you serve moose here?"

She didn't look at me when she asked the question.

The waitress said, "Our chocolate pudding is very close, it's quite light."

"No," Anna said, "I mean the animal moose."

"We really just have the small finger sandwiches," the waitress said. "Watercress, cucumber, tomahto, shrimp, cucumber—"

"Because, if a moose walks in here and is seated," Anna continued, "I will have to leave."

It was at that moment I realized that I had been played. Perfectly.

I laughed. Anna laughed. We couldn't stop laughing. We both sat there shaking like Pentecostals.

The waitress walked away.

I don't remember if we actually ate lunch.

. . . . .

Anna and I have been friends from that day on. And I must admit, I need friends. I've always needed friends. Sometimes, I feel like a walking donut; I have this big hole right through me. I suspected for a long while that I spoke a strange language that nobody understood. That I saw things they didn't. And I wondered if anyone outside of this town might relate. There's nothing but relics here.

Anna is one of the few girls I can relate to. Oh, so smart. (Am I repeating myself?) Oh, so funny. I love funny. (Yes, I'm repeating myself.) She's become a big sister, friend, and sometimes co-conspirator. After my lunch date with Anna, I had started living with a silent fear that she and my brother would break up and I'd lose her.

But friend or not, Anna is Friday's. I needed—really needed, desperately wanted, desired, longed for, hoped for—someone for me. Please, someone who gets what I say instead of looking at me like I just dropped from outer space. Better yet, put me back on my planet with my own people.

I kept waiting for my flying saucer to come in. When it finally did, it landed right on my heart.

eight

I Love You
(Wait, I didn't mean it.)

After the suicide chat—when I had asked Carolina to tell the story of her wrist-slash— she and I started visiting Mandelo's Harley Davidson regularly. Whenever she straddled one of those machines, I got that movie urge to grab her, hold her in my arms, and kiss her while the music hits all the B-movie melodrama chords and the light fades just before the credits roll. If I were a boy, maybe I would've kissed her there in Mandelo's. But I'm not, so I didn't. What was I supposed to do?

Is this love, or what? I wondered.

I decided to discuss the issue with Em's old—my new—typewriter. The shop was closed so I brought it down to the donut counter. The keys snapped out my thoughts.

Dear Carolina,

I love you, wait, I didn't mean it, I mean how can I love you, I hardly even know you, I mean I can't love you this quickly, not really, we've talked, you said that people say I love you but I love you is only a bunch of words easier to say but not so easy to do and maybe it's going to take a while to figure out but that's okay we'll take the time when we're ready we can really say I love you but I won't say it now, well, I did, but I didn't mean it, no, I meant, I like you, I like you a lot, I like you a whole lot, I like you immensely, big time, you're really cool, but I can't say I love you no, not yet, so if it slips sometimes, at a moment when I'm not thinking so clearly about the true meaning of true love, if I just blurt out an I love you I just mean I love you as much as a person can love someone in such a short time, that's what I mean, so if I say I love you please know that perhaps at that crazy second I feel something very close to love, a Xerox, or Silly Putty on the comics copy of love, but not the real thing, no that's impossible at this place and time, so if those words slip out please know that it's no big thing.

    Maybe.

I don't know.

Sincerely, your lover, T—

Wait, did I type "lover?" Oh, man.

Maybe I'll show Carolina my letter.

And maybe the square donuts will make me a millionaire. (Fat chance.)

•

H e r   H a b i t   o f   L e a v i n g

Home of the square donut with the amazing pink icing.

Yeah. Now, I don't want to bite the hairy hand that feeds me, but as I told you, I like my donuts like I like most things—to have substance. A cake donut is thick, dense, and meaty, soft on the inside, slightly crisp on the out. It's made to be eaten warm (not hot) from the fryer, preferably with a glass of cold milk or, in the fall, a paper cup of apple cider. And when it comes to looks, the traditional round cake donut, in my humble opinion, is, well, perfect. Put two on a plate, donut on donut, the one on top slightly askew, add the aforementioned ice-cold glass of milk or a cup of coffee served in traditional thick diner ware, and you have a work of art as good as anything I've ever seen on a field trip to the Cleveland Museum of Art. Bite into a cake donut at The Precinct Donut Emporium and you have tasted art, which is something you cannot do downtown. Now, with this in mind, you may understand how I came to reject the notion of the square donut with the amazing pink icing.

True, I've grown up with this donut. I've seen it from day one, so it isn't a matter of snubbing something new. It just so happened that one day, when I was still a kid, I saw that it was just plain wrong. Square around a circle. No. Pink icing. Why? It doesn't taste like cherry. It doesn't taste like strawberry. It's a plain old confectioner's sugar and water glaze. It's not a sugar, butter, and milk glaze. It's not a butter, milk, and corn syrup glaze. Sugar, water, and red food coloring, period. Watered down red food coloring, at that. The square donut with the amazing pink icing. Huh. The only thing that saves its sweet little self is that it's a yeast donut. The yeast donut, though popular, is all fluff. So if one were going to bastardize a donut, this is the donut to bastardize.

So, you wonder—*what's her point?*

My point is: I've never told my dad this. I've avoided making the donuts. I've purposely goofed them up. I've dropped the dough on the floor. Forgotten the yeast or added too much. Over-fried. Made blood-red icing. I've done everything except face my dad with the truth: "Your square donut isn't amazing, it's stupid!" Even when I've had the chance, even when he once said to me, "Bee, you seem to have a mental block when making the square donuts." I smiled and said, "I guess you're the only one who can make them, Dad. No one makes them like you do." He smiled and patted my head. And I've never had to make a square donut again.

The point of my point is this: The deeper I feel about something the less I can talk about it. Even when I want to talk, I pray for distraction so I don't have to talk. I yelled about the woods that I feel passionate about because the guy I was yelling at meant nothing to me. But when somebody means something to me....

So, ever since Carolina spoke of her habit of leaving—which I refer to in my head as the "Rolling Stone Gathers No Crap" speech—I've been shaky. Which is weird because, basically, I expect people to leave. I don't mean to be a wimp; I just figure it's going to happen. Seems like every time I've had a best friend, somebody I really liked to hang with, they'd move. It's happened no less than three times—Ronnie Schafer in the fifth grade, Mary Beth Evans in the seventh, and Becca Fishburger in the ninth. Sure, I had other kids to hang with, but it's about finding the best—the one you really click with, the one you don't even have to talk to because you already know what she's thinking, the best of the best. *My* bests all moved away. And then there's Mitch. Gone, gone, gone. And hey, when you can't even get your mom to stay when you're two, just about the cutest age a kid can be...Lord, that sounds so pitiful. Excuse me while I suffer.

Anyway, Carolina's the best of the best of the best. Man, we hardly need to talk at all, just be. If my favorite rock at the beach were a human with a cute butt, it'd be her.

So, ever since Carolina spoke of her habit of leaving, damn, I can't take it. I've never wanted to hold onto anybody so much in my life. I need her. I breathe in, she breathes out. The blood flows out of my left ventricle and into her right ventricle, or however that works; you get my drift. That's how it feels. I know it's all too much. It's so dependent. I need her and I know I need her and I know that need is going to make her go away. I know it. I know it. I know it. God, I could empty my own veins right now.

Why do I feel this way? It's a pain. It's too intense. I love intense. I hate intense. I make love to her in tents. I feel like an idiot. I am an idiot. I'm an idiot. Stop feeling this way. Stop it, stop it, stop it. I can't stop it. I want to be her Siamese twin. One body, one heart. Is that love, or am I just pitiful? Don't tell me. I don't even want to know what I already know. I try to be cool, to keep those feelings down so that I don't make her go away. I don't want to suffocate her. She'd be out of here faster than a bulldozer can take down a 150-year-old maple. That's fast. Can I get a witness?

Carolina sleeps in my bed with me almost every night. I don't know what my dad thinks. Does he think we're having a PJ party? Because believe me, there's not a pajama between us. I don't know what he sees. What he hears. What he feels. He's always been so quiet and so weird. I feel guilty pulling the wool over his eyes. I want to talk to him. I don't want to talk to him. How would I? *Excuse me, Dad, I just want to thank you for letting my girlfriend move into my bedroom. We're having great sex!*

If I can't talk donuts with him, I can't talk about my love life. I want to talk to him about my mother. I want to talk to him and I can't stand the thought of talking to him. Most of all, I don't want to do anything that'd take away my Carolina. Did I call her "my" Carolina? See what I mean? I'm pitiful.

When I feel this way, I try to think of her imperfections. Like, when I get up, the stars are just leaving, but the sun is old by the time Carolina pokes her size $9\frac{1}{2}$ narrows into her cowboy boots. She lies around a lot. I come from a long line of working stiffs. We work hard and save all our money. It's what we do. Sometimes I hate us for working so much, so I try not to lay it on Carolina. Most days, when she finally rolls out from under the percale, she'll help me clean up if it means getting out faster. I must say, though, she's not much of a stickler when it comes to cleanliness. Her idea of mopping the floor is moving a dishrag around with her toe while talking. Or kissing (which works for me). And why use soap when a good rinse will do? Board of Health, screw 'em, we've got better things to do—like talk with our hands. I read her lips. I close my eyes. I'm blind. All other senses are amplified. I finger her Braille goosebumps. They all spell, "I'm perfection."

t e n

Cold Coffee

Loss is life. Loss of life is life. Loss of life stinks. When they found what was left of Mitch—parts of him, not the whole Mitch, his dog tags and enough to identify him with whatever magic formula they use to turn bone and flesh into a "positive ID" so they can knock on your door and tell you what a hero he was. Some people said it was a relief in a sense, knowing for sure.

But me? I was real attached to my fantasy that Mitch had escaped to a remote island with some exotic-looking woman and was spawning a hut full of exotic-looking babies that he was going to bring home any day now. He'd drive them all around in his Camaro, and they'd come to The Precinct and I'd make them cream puffs, and they would love those cream puffs because they were just like their dad.

I didn't cry right away when I first heard; I was too ticked off, thinking of him suffering all alone there, all alone. Stupid. Just stupid how he's gone. The farthest east he'd ever been was Pennsylvania for a dirt bike race. The closest he'd been to Asia was a can of LaChoy Chicken Chow Mein. Stupid.

The day we buried Mitch was one of the most beautiful ever, eighty-two degrees, sunny blue sky, a warm breeze. If I were running things, all funerals would be on gray, drizzly days. Damp and cold. Days that match the hurt you feel inside. I watched Auntie Flo. I don't think she had used her Miller method; she was just sobbing full tilt, straight from crush in her chest. I thought she was going to throw herself on top of the casket and beg to be lowered into the ground with her son. I saw Uncle Nick differently that day. He was typically quiet, sure, like steel is quiet. He seemed tall and strong, holding his wife like he was going to be there forever and never let her go. Otherwise, I think she really would have taken a swan dive into that grave.

I studied my dad, Hush Brother #2, right there next to Nick and Flo. Could Friday possibly be standing any closer to him? And Anna, a gold halo of sun reflecting off her hair, sewn to Friday. The Ems, Emily with her rumpled suit and sensible shoes, Emaline in her bohemia wear. All together, locked tight like they were about to play Red Rover. Nothing was going to break them apart. Even Carolina was edging in close to the pack.

An Army guy gave my Aunt a flag, a bugle played "Taps," young soldiers respectfully gave my dead war hero cousin a nine-gun salute. Every time I heard a shot, I felt like the bullet went through my brain. Maybe, at that moment, I wished it would. I felt like my head was buzzing. Numb. Like I hadn't slept and was catching a cold.

My legs felt weak. I don't remember much about the wake, but lots of people brought food. There were people from the Army, veterans from other wars, and friends and neighbors. People who supported the war and those who didn't grieved just the same.

The wake was at the donut shop, where Kasper and Min took charge. I sat in a booth and let my coffee get cold. I didn't want any warm-ups. Cold coffee, it seemed to me, was the fitting drink after my cousin's funeral.

eleven

Found Alive

Before Mitch wasn't here anymore, when he wasn't here and missing, we still held onto the possibility of his someday being here. I guess that's called hope. Hope is what saves you, even if it's for a snip at a time. Carolina's hope came in the shape of a motorcycle, which eventually brought her here. Whatever shape it comes in, I suspect hope is the big lie you tell yourself to get you from one place to the next.

I wonder how many other lies I've been telling me. Me. I always thought of myself as honest. Now, there's this Carolina wool I'm pulling over my dad's and everybody else's eyes. I've got a very sticky Maraschino sitting on top of one whopping hot fudge sundae of a lie. I'm in love with a girl, okay? No, it's not, no it's not, no it's not. But oh, I am, oh I am, oh I am. And to make things worse, here I am, sentenced for life to the damned donut shop.

Is this why I went to kindergarten? Is this why I learned my ABCs? Well, I'll tell you what I think of me. I go through elementary school on into junior high, then high school, and I learn and I study, breezing through spelling bees and SATs, which I only took because I had the twenty bucks. For what? Donuts. Capital D-O-N-U-T-S. Donuts. Which rhymes with "go nuts."

If I were you, I'd tell me to get myself up and leave if it's so godforsaken unbearable. That's what I'd tell me if I were in your shoes. But there are some pieces missing from this jigsaw. You know how my mom left, but I didn't tell you about Friday.

You know I love Friday's girl, Anna. I even love her name, because it makes just all kinds of sense. It's simple and to the point and has a beautiful sound. You can spell it backward and forward and it's beautiful just the same. Well, Anna and Friday were going to get married. They were making all kinds of plans for a wedding, including having me as a bridesmaid—well, maid of honor, which I would not tolerate except for the fact that it would be for Friday and Anna.

Those two were all excited about getting married and running the donut shop, which would get me off the donut hook. Only one day, Anna had a seizure, which led to the knowledge that she had a brain tumor. All the doctors got together and operated, only to find out they were too late. So, they closed her head back up and shook theirs. She's on all kinds of drugs that make her a little slower, but she's still amazing and funny and…I love her and we love her.

Once, she told me a story about how she wet her bed until she was eleven. She was all serious and sad about it, so to cheer her up, I wrote her a ditty and read it to her.

<u>Ode to a Bed Wetter</u>

Anna used to hang her head,
Cause Anna used to wet her bed.
Every night poor Ann would dread,
Another puddle on the spread.
She longed to wake up in the john,
Instead of turning bed to pond.
She wished she had a magic wand
To keep from being peed upon.
Nights with her unwelcome guest
Put our loved one to the test.
Though always hoping for the best,
She'd wake to find she'd messed her nest.
Then one day to her surprise,
She rose from bed with covers dry.
Shouting with a joyful cry.
"I didn't pee the bed! I didn't pee the bed!"

It was a dumb ditty, but Anna laughed until she nearly peed her pants, which, of course, was the perfect response.

It's been a little while now with this brain tumor thing, and she's going in and out of remembering who's who and what's what. She's quite sick. One morning, she didn't know who Friday was, and that about killed him. Later that day, she knew him. She's about over, and it's killing us all.

I don't mean to be so selfish right now as to bring this all back to me, but really, how can I leave? My dad's had years to get over my so-called mother leaving him— which he hasn't exactly done, but if you ask me, he's stretching it out a little too far. It's become a way of life for him to be bitter about being left. They were together for about six whole years; she's been gone more than twice that. I figure, hey, get over it.

I could leave if it was just him. But Friday, I don't know if you've caught on, I think he's pretty okay.

After that day, if you remember—the day I told you about when Carolina kissed me in front of him—well, Friday didn't say much to me, which was highly unusual. He's never been a bossy brother, but he doesn't mind giving his honest opinion of my behavior. As a matter of fact, I've never known him to be shy about telling me exactly what he thinks. He usually finds just the right words to express himself and plenty of them, so this silence on the subject of the Carolina kiss, compounded by the Carolina move-in, was a new thing. I found it unnerving.

I was bracing myself for the damtobreakthebomb togooffallhelltoletloosetheothershoetodropandtheshitto hitthefan, but it kept on not happening. Sometime after Carolina's lippy exposé and after the "clipboard incident," as the encounter with the man in hardhat bulldozing the woods came to be known, but before we found out that Mitch was definitely dead and before Anna didn't remember that Friday was Friday. Back in the brief space in time when who I was sleeping with mattered somehow, back before death sneaked in a pulled rank on sex, Friday said his piece to me. I could tell he'd given it a lot of thought, but gave me the condensed version.

"Regarding Carolina," he said, "I think you two are okay." Then he shrugged. That was it. Boom. Period. It was the end of the subject—and the beginning of something very new.

twelve

Pre-Carolina, I wasn't so very happy, was I? I'll answer that: no. I am kind of feeling kind of better now, though. A lot less like a donut. (And a lot more like a tart. Ha, ha.) But I still had this gnawing, nagging thing. This tugging, bugging thing.

Then one night, Friday got all spiffed up and left for a date with Anna. The next thing I knew, he was back at the door with a very pretty, all dressed-up Anna, and she said to me and Carolina, "What are you guys doing tonight?"

She lumped us together, like two being one. I looked at Carolina as her shoulders gave a "not much" shrug, and Anna said, "Come with us on a double date, okay? We're going to dinner."

A double *date*.

Friday said we needed to wear something that wasn't jeans, so we got changed real quick and joined the fiancés on their date.

They took us to the Brown Derby, a pricey steakhouse. Friday bought. We laughed and we talked and we were so included. So included in a public place. That's when happy came to me. It washed over me like a warm bath. Carolina and I were together, close and something. We were something. We were a unit. We were a couple, and it felt legitimate. Legitimate—I did not know exactly what I was missing until Friday and Anna wrapped up a heaping helping of acceptance with a steak and a baked potato and handed it to me.

I knew I wanted more of it. So often, I felt like everybody else was walking right foot first, and I was starting with my left out. Yeah, left out.

Left out because I didn't have a mom. Left out because, while other little girls were joining Brownies, I was busy taking them out of the oven. Or because my dad had Min tell me about my period, and she wasn't around when I couldn't figure out how to use a tampon. And maybe because the person trying to help me learn to use makeup was Auntie Flo, who applied hers with a putty knife and had to remove it with a Brillo pad. And not only was that a scary experience, when she was through with me, I looked like a clown geisha country music singer, but she had no ear for the fact that I was not interested in makeup or hair teasing. And maybe, *maybe* a person's mom would have understood that.

And maybe I felt sorry for my dad. Pitied him, even, because I could see that he was trying. And maybe lots of people are nice and kind to me, but they never see me. And maybe I'd like to be seen and maybe, just maybe, for the first time, on a double date with my girlfriend and my brother and his fianceé, I felt normal and calm and easy and happy. And that night, I wasn't mad and I didn't hate anyone or anything. I just felt good.

Then Anna made an announcement.

"They're going to do some more surgery on me, guys. And I think I'll be okay, so the wedding's still on schedule, you know."

"She's going to be great," Friday said, stroking her hair. "She's going to be perfect."

I looked at my brother, puzzled. I thought that the doctors had already closed the case. His eyes were sad, and he gave me a "just go with it" nod. Carolina saw it, too.

"Oh, we know you're going to be fine, Anna," Carolina said. "I met this guy on the road once, he had a brain tumor removed, and he was, like, you wouldn't know."

Anna was smiling. "And we want kids, lots of them," she said.

Friday was smiling. "We love kids."

"And you guys will be like the new Ems," Anna said.

"The new Ems," I repeated. "I hope we can be as good as Ems as the Ems are."

"You will be," Anna said. "I know it."

And I wished it could be true.

thirteen

The Law of Gravity

I didn't learn much back in physics class, but in life, I have learned two important things:

1. When you're up, there's no place to go but down.
2. Gravity keeps your feet on the ground.

As an illustration of point number one, I was with my girl, my love, hanging out on the couch in the apartment. I was perusing my *Hollywood Stars* magazine, still floating high and all I said was, "Do you think it's the gray lake water that flushes the personality out of everyone who lives in this town?"

And Carolina, who had just finished removing her toenail polish said, "God, Toby, why are you so down on this place? People here are really nice." She screwed the top back on the toenail polish remover and tossed three pungent, red-smirched wet cotton balls into a waste basket. She shrugged her shoulders at me to emphasize "why?"

Huh?

"Maybe the reason you feel alienated is because you alienate yourself."

What? "I was just saying—"

"You were just all depressie-sorry for yourself …again," she said. Which made me kind of angry. And my anger might have stayed in the "kind of" stage if she had stopped. But no, she said to me (and I'm putting this into my own words here as best as I remember it): "Toby, your life is not so bad. You have a family that loves you, really loves you. I think you expect too much and make them work too hard. You can be a lot of work."

My love was telling me things I did not wish to hear, so I said, "What do you know about work? I haven't seen you lift a finger since you plopped down here."

She lifted a finger to show me she could.

"Oh, nice," I said, before careening recklessly forward. "And by the way, you are no easy task yourself. You ran around naked at the beach like this is some kind of nudist colony, which it is not. What if people saw you? I mean you were just naked and everything." (I pulled that one out of the bottom of the bag.) "And you don't work. I mean, you do help, sometimes, but the fact of the matter is, you don't clean very well."

There, I thought.

"You can't take criticism, can you?" she asked flatly.

Wait a minute—I had just turned the tables. How'd it get back to me so fast?

"Yeah, I can, but shut up. I can. I can take it when it's constructive, and—"

"I was constructive," she interrupted, even more flatly.

"No, you were just critical. Critical, like a critic who's…critical."

Okay, I was redundant, but I was under pressure.

"I said you feel sorry for yourself too much," she countered.

If I could have taken a carpenter's level to her tone at that moment, the bubble would have been smack in the middle. Level. Flat, flat, flat. My irritation level, on the other hand, was quite off the bubble.

"That's your opinion. That's…." My frustration level leapt to join my irritation, which met my voice a few octaves higher.

"And sometimes you're hard to live with," she added. "You're so defensive."

"Yeah, right, defensive. I'm defensive."

"I'm glad you agree," she said, smiling at my last nerve.

"What? You just sit around here all day thinking of these things, maybe you should find something else to do," I said.

"Hey, it doesn't take a lot of time to see how sorry you feel for yourself. Aw, I'm wasting my breath."

"No, you wouldn't want to waste your breath, you might need it to lay around…and…and…paint your toenails and stuff!" I half-yelled as she walked out of the room and down the back steps.

Oh, how clever was my last line, ringing in my ears. Feeling sorry for myself, ha! Defensive, ha! Ha! Ha! Ha! That girl has no idea. No idea. No. She can just stomp down those stairs, walk herself to the beach, dive off the edge of the earth and drop to the bottom of the Great Stink Lake and never surface.

Headline: "Young Drifter Disappears Off Shore of Old Beach."

No.

"Erie Disappearance. Young, Unemployed, Do-Nothing Know-It-All Sinks like Rock to Bottom of Great Lake, Never to Return."

No.

"Erie Disappearance. Young, Unemployed Drifter Do-Nothing Know-It-All with Flat Tone Who, Even When She Lifts a Finger Doesn't Know the Meaning of

Cleaning a Kitchen or Anything for that Matter, Sinks Titanically to the Depths of the Great Lake Erie."

Subhead: Experts predict her body will never be recovered. No one grieves.

I sat, stewing and stewing and stewing.

Defensive/sorry/defensive/sorry/defensive/sorry. Then, I started feeling sorry for myself. Then, I got defensive. Then, I knew she was right. Maybe. Then, I hated her for maybe being right. Then, it got late and she wasn't back. Where was she? I got into bed and put my hand on the pillow where her head wasn't. Then I started feeling sorry for myself. Then I became angry that I was feeling sorry for myself, so I stomped out of the house and down the back steps. I stood and looked around, then headed for the beach. What if she did throw herself in? I walked faster. *You'd better damned be at the damned beach, Carolina,* I thought. *Please.*

I squeezed through the fence and sat there on my rock. Then I walked up and down, and then sat on that rock again until my butt got cold. (Even after 20,000 summers, that rock holds the memory of the ice age in its belly.) Finally, I went home to bed, where Carolina lay sleeping.

"Hey, where were you?" I hissed, feeling justified in my anger.

"Hummm...?" She stirred.

I poked at her. "Hey, where were you?"

"Ummm, what? Hi."

"What do you mean, 'What hi'? Where were you?"

"Are you still mad?" she asked.

"I might be. Definitely. Sort of."

In truth, I was more scared than angry. In truth, I had moments of panic while I was sitting on that rock.

She was silent. I continued, tired. "I don't know." My voice was going soft on me.

"You sound all mushy."

"Shut up. Where were you?" I repeated.

"I can't tell you where I was if I shut up," she literalized.

I ran out of words.

"Okay," she said. "I was at The Tavern, having a pop with Friday."

"With Friday?"

"Yeah, we had a very good, very long conversation."

"About what?" What I really meant was, "About me?" But I didn't say it.

"You're lucky to have him for a brother. You are lucky to have this family."

I felt like the BUNN-O-Matic was doing a slow drip on my forehead.

"Yeah, I know, but what did you talk about?" Translation: What were you guys saying about me?

"We didn't talk about you," she ESP'd. "We just bullshitted."

Bullshit.

"And you don't know," Carolina continued, "you don't know how good you've got it. You have everything."

Everything? I didn't get it. How could I have everything? I live above a donut shop. I'm a waitress and a counter mopper and a coffee pourer and a big fat liar and, um, a lesbian. Oh, that word. Who made up that horrible-sounding word? I was suddenly exhausted, and my butt was really cold. I got into bed next to her warm self and tried to make out the cracks in the ceiling. In the dim, the big one looked like Noah's ark.

"Carolina, do you really think I have everything?"

"I do."

"But my mom ...."

"You should see mine," she said, yawning and turning on her side, throwing her arm around my waist, indicating that I needed to turn on my side so that we would be in our regular sleeping position. I did, grateful to burrow my bottom into her warm belly. Grateful she still wanted me there.

"Maybe you're better off with no mom than one that is so screwed up that she screws your life up."

"And this town ...." I continued.

"Toby, you're hopeless," she said. "And your butt's cold."

"Really?" I asked.

"Yeah, it's freezing," she said.

"No." I felt anxious. "I'm hopeless?"

"God, Toby." She sighed, paused, and then added, "You're far from hopeless." She climbed on top of me and sat on my belly, putting her hands on my shoulders. She looked me straight in the eyes. "You're a really good person. You're kind of spoiled, but you and your family are good people. I always imagined there were people like you, I just never met any before."

"Really?"

"Really."

"I'm sorry about what I said about you not cleaning very well," I said. "Even though it's true."

We both laughed.

"But, I did rethink one thing," I said. "I actually liked you naked on the beach. It's one of the best memories I have. You should do it more often."

"You never know," she said.

She was right, I did never know.

She slid off my belly, and we resumed our earlier spoon position.

I remembered again the conversation she'd had with Anna, Min, and me that day, about her habit of leaving.

Be naked, be dressed, just be here.

And as if she had again heard my thought, she moved her hand to my cheek, resting it there as she fell into sleep.

As I felt her sweet self against me, tears started pushing out of my ducts. *Damn. Is this feeling sorry for myself?* I wondered.

I wondered into a fog, out of which walked Anna. Dear Anna, who so wants to live and get married and have children that she has imagined an impossible surgery.

I thought about the ache I feel inside of me when I worry about Carolina leaving.

I thought about the ache that Friday must feel when he thinks of Anna leaving. I finally felt the ache I feel when I think of Anna leaving, when I think of her dying. I hadn't really experienced what the thought of her dying felt like. I was hoping so much that she wouldn't, believing so much she wouldn't, that I had not let myself know that she might. I had that kind of hope for Mitch, but look what happened. I started feeling sorry for Anna. How scared she must be. Maybe it's lonely to be surrounded by people who don't want to think about you dying. Maybe she didn't want to think about it, or maybe she did. And if she did, was there anyone she could talk to about what was real to her? I started crying. I started sobbing. Carolina woke up.

"What's the matter?"

"Anna."

"Anna," she repeated, and of course, started crying. It wasn't just her reflex. If you knew Anna, you'd have cried, too.

We cried for Anna and we cried for Mitch and we cried for each other, and probably for a whole bunch of stuff we didn't know we were crying about. And we made love. We were awake talking and crying and making love. All night.

Somehow, being surrounded by death, I felt more alive than I ever had.

Yeah, there's nothing like gravity to pull your feet right to the ground.

f o u r t e e n

Forbidden Fruit Pies

Okay, it's not that I did anything wrong. I did it way back when I was in grade school, when I was a kid, when I had to have them: Hostess Twinkies, cupcakes, and fruit pies.

In our house, it was blasphemy, and I knew it. I could get fresh-baked sweets at any time. Donuts, popovers, fritters, cream puffs, all made with real ingredients. No artificial anything, no preservatives, nothing but pure sugars and fats. But I was tempted by the Hostess in those cute little packages, cellophane and waxed paper with little loving hearts. And the treat itself, the bottom of which would inevitably stick to the white paper tray that cradled it, and would need to be scraped off with my teeth.

I used to trade for Hostess. My dad didn't know. Not a clue. Two fresh-that-morning chocolate-covered donuts for a Twinkie. A bear claw for a fruit pie. I don't know why I feel it's important to mention, I just do. Maybe what the donut laureate says is true: confection is good for the soul.

. . . . .

So, we were just sitting there at the old beach, Carolina and I, a day or two after the argument that led to an even closer closeness, that reached beyond anything I could have imagined. We were just sitting there, watching the waves slap at the rocks, watching the lake spit up between the breakers, studying the gray water blending into the gray sky. It even smelled gray that day. I felt close to her, so I finally asked, "So, why haven't you told me about yourself? From Detroit?"

She hit at her cigarette pack and pulled one out, tapped it on her hand, and put it in her mouth. She was sitting with her knees bent, her pant legs rolled above her ankles, sand on her feet, the red polish on her toes all scraped up. She lit her cigarette with a lighter this time, snapping it shut real tough and moody. She took a drag and spoke, looking at the horizon instead of me.

"Because you like the mystery," she said. Then she looked at me.

"You didn't want to know anything about me, Toby. You didn't want to know me. You just wanted me to be this exciting mystery lover. The forbidden one. The one to save you from what you perceive as your stupid, boring life."

She sounded so matter-of-fact. My reaction, as usual, was to feel all sorry wondering where my hold-me-while-I-cry sweet lover went. And kicking myself for ruining things somehow. I tried to pull myself out.

"I love you, Carolina." Yeah, I said it. I said it out loud. But when I said it, I was bummed because it came out sob-like.

"Yeah," she said.

I sank as she looked back at the horizon and finished her cigarette in silence. My stomach was stone. I felt wet and gray. I wanted to take back this conversation and make it all really cool again. I couldn't move. I was afraid if I moved, she'd say she had to be going. Like when someone's over and you don't want them to leave. You're afraid that if you offer them a drink, you'll remind them that they're still there, and they'll say they'd better get home, so you don't offer them anything hoping they'll stay longer. I was afraid if I moved, she'd be gone. I remained still, too scared to think.

She sat staring out forever before turning back to me. "I don't know what love is, Toby, but I do like being here with you."

I could breathe again. This girl from Detroit, who had no suitcases and a truckload of baggage, might just stay for a while. The girl who was wise, the girl who was crazy, the girl I was hot for 98.6% of the time.

Yeah, she has these sides. Side A was the kind of mature from having seen the world. Her flip Side B was kind of wild and unpredictable. That side made an accidental suicide attempt. That side sat naked on the beach. That side kissed me in front of Friday. That side took a joyride on Officer Wheedle's motorcycle.

Now, Officer Wheedle is an anal-retentive, just-the-facts-ma'am, go-by-the-book-and-throw-it-at-'em-while-you're-at-it kind of cop. He arrived at The Precinct (Donut Emporium) every morning at six sharp, where his two jelly-filled and coffee with cream were waiting, warm and ready. At six twenty-three, he'd take his last gulp of joe, wipe a paper napkin across his bloated face, put his buck and quarter down, slap on his hat, and John Wayne out to his motorcycle. He'd then take his two-minute ride up to the station, dismount, tug at his privates, and walk in at precisely six twenty-five, a full five minutes before duty began. He was a loyal and serious thirty-four-year-old bachelor. A career cop. His job was to uphold the law, and he did it with all the sincerity of a child and intellectual maturity to match.

We all knew that the joy of Officer Wheedle's life was his Harley Davidson, a cherry-red Fat Boy, which is also a fairly apt description of Officer Wheedle. I loved and adored Officer Wheedle's motorcycle. Officer Wheedle? Well, all other feelings aside, I can't help but kind of respect the guy. Nobody really wants to be the world's biggest asshole, but he got the job, and I must admit he does it well.

This one morning, Officer Wheedle came in per usual, when the hands on the clock face were as straight and sharp as the stick up his butt. He plopped down on a stool, plumped his fleshy pointer into the ring of his ceramic mug, and was about to take his first gulp of the day when his ears lifted to the unmistakable musical sound of a Harley Davidson revving up. In a flash, that officer was on the case and at the door. We all followed just in time to catch a glimpse of Carolina sitting on that leather seat, wearing cowboy boots, cutoff long johns, a t-shirt, and a smile much too big for the time of day.

Officer Wheedle ran out to his baby, and I stared at mine, thinking how sexy she looked as she cranked it up, let it out, and took off. Then, everybody turned around and started yelling at *me*.

Officer Wheedle was foaming, cursing and spitting. There were a couple other men there in the near-dark, walking around and kicking gravel. They discussed and concluded that a chase was not the best solution, and decide to wait it out. Meanwhile, I heard words like "little bitch" and threats of bodily harm if a scratch appeared anywhere on the precious metal of that bike. Its beauty began to fade for me. I watched the men stand helplessly by as Officer Wheedle threw his little man-fit.

Minutes crawled before I heard the distant purr of the Harley, then the crunch of the driveway. The men scattered as Carolina skidded up, smiling an incredibly fake smile. I was hoping she'd get all Evel Knievel and pop a wheelie over their heads, but she didn't.

Officer Wheedle stomped up to her, looking like he was going to rip her like a donut. She stuck out her hand to shake his, still smiling. He smacked it away as he bulldozed past, inspecting his beloved bike.

I heard Carolina say, "Officer Wheedle, you have such a wonderful machine here. You cannot blame me for wanting a ride. It must be such a rush to have so much power between one's legs."

I gasped.

Officer Wheedle called her an obnoxious little brat. He said something about how he should arrest her and if she knew what they did to girls in jail.

Satisfied that his bike survived, and I think somewhat embarrassed, he climbed up and left for work. It was exactly six twenty-three as he took off down the street. No time had been lost.

I yelled, "Thank you for coming to The Precinct Donut Emporium, home of the square donut with the amazing pink icing." Then I looked around to see that

Carolina had already disappeared. I glanced at my dad and did a double-take. It was still kind of dark, but I swear he was smiling.

. . . . .

So, anyway, out of the blue, Carolina announced that she took a job at the Texaco station—pumping gas, for God's sake. She said she wanted to earn her keep and contribute to things around the house. She said it over dinner. It was her and me and dad. She looked right at him and added, "If you don't mind my staying, Mr. Renfrew."

My dad blushed a little—kind of odd for him, that show of emotion. He cleared his throat and said that she was welcome, that she was part of the family. Carolina misted up then as their eyes locked. My mouth hung open, full of half-chewed Swiss steak and tater tots. Who was this man and what was going on here?

I swallowed, looked at my dad, and smiled, sort of. Then I looked at Carolina. I knew that I should always never know what to expect, yet I'm always surprised when the unexpected happens. This little interchange between her and my dad...when did they connect, and how?

He really liked her; it was obvious. Did he know about us? What did he know about us? When I realized how much he liked her, I felt guilty for just about everything to do with us.

After dinner, Carolina and I were doing the dishes. I was washing and she was doing a terrible job rinsing and drying. Dad was in his Lazyboy, watching Dan Rather lather. I said, "I can't believe my dad. Wow."

"Yeah," she said, "he's really cool."

"Once in a while," I said, still stunned. "And a job? When did you start looking for a job?"

"You said I should work. I listened."

"I was mad when I said that."

"But you were right."

"Yeah, but what about...I hope it doesn't interfere with...us," I whispered, looking toward the thin blue light of the living room.

"What about us?" she teased.

"Sex," I whispered emphatically.

My dad was usually gone most afternoons, fishing or harping with his cronies, so we had an empty house for a couple hours until dinnertime. And we knew how to use it.

"We'll make time," she said. "So to speak." She smiled, raising her eyebrows.

I smiled back, unsure. I thumped the dishes around in the sink, thinking for a while. Then I asked frenetically, "You working to stay, or working to go? I've got to know, are you getting the money to live here or leave?"

She squinted, as if trying to see into the deep leftfield I was coming out of.

"I just want to pay my way around here. Besides, I need money. I've run out."

"Run out." The words stuck like bubblegum to my brain, and I chewed them in silence, my dishrag keeping time. Run out. Run out. Run out.

"You're paranoid, Toby."

"You're the one who said a rolling stone gathers no crap."

She started laughing. "A rolling stone gathers no crap. That's funny. Did Kasper say that?"

"That's what you said."

"What are you talking about?"

"You said it in the shop to me and Min and Anna. You said, 'A rolling stone gathers no crap,' like you were the fucking rolling stone and like I was the crap! Geezus, I fucking said fucking. Fuck. Goddammit." I was having a curse-a-thon.

"I don't remember saying that."

"Geezus, you don't fucking remember saying that? I have based everything about us on that one statement, like any second you would be rolling right out of here, and you don't fucking remember saying it? You were all cool and serious and blowing smoke out of the side of your mouth. Like, 'oh, I'm a rolling stone.' Geezus, Carolina. Shit."

She shook her head, glanced over her shoulder toward the dozing old man, then led me to the top of the back steps with the hand not holding the checkered dish towel and sudsy plate.

Half-laughing she said, "I'm sorry. I'm such an ass, Toby."

"Yeah, yeah you are. Oh my God. Dammit, Carolina—"

"Stop it." She kissed me.

"Geezus—"

"Stop it." She kissed me again.

I stopped it and kissed her back.

"Damn…" I faded.

In my mind, I wanted a document, a legal contract, written—no, chiseled in stone—no, in 24-karat gold, 25- if they have it. A legal contract in gold, chiseled by Moses, cosigned by God, notarized by Mother Theresa, witnessed by a stadium full of lawyers, the entire United States Supreme Court, all of their aunties, Up With People, and a whole goddamned troop of Eagle Scouts. Her contract, her promise that she would never ever leave me, ever.

I didn't think it was too much to ask.

. . . . .

Life went on. Me and my girlfriend living with my dad and my brother. We were becoming a family, and I was beginning to feel less awkward about it. We got to the point where we were laughing at the dinner table. Even Friday laughed, a rare sound since the Anna situation, which, by the way, was only racing downhill.

What I loved most was the feeling of Carolina's body next to mine, the faint liaison of gasoline and Safeguard lingering on her skin. On my lips. She really was making me forget how miserable my life was.

One night, while I was enjoying the sweet warmth of her, Carolina said in a kind of innocent way, "I think Officer Wheedle is making the moves on me."

She may as well have spit hot grease in my face. I sat straight up in bed, jerking like a marionette, and yelled, "What?"

"Christ!" she yelled back.

We stared at each other for a minute, or at least I assume we did, it being dark in the room. Then I said, "I will kill him."

"God, Toby," she said, as if it was no big deal.

"What'd he do?" I demanded.

"It's no big deal," she said. (What'd I tell you?) "I'm sorry I mentioned it."

I jumped out of bed, so angry I had to pace while giving her the third degree. "What'd he do? Did he touch you? He touched you, didn't he? Did he molest you?" I didn't wait for answers, the questions being somewhat rhetorical. "What the hell, Carolina? This guy's got to be stopped. I've got to do something."

"Like what, exactly?" Carolina asked, a little too amused.

"It's not funny, this is serious," I said, although I hadn't stopped to find out exactly what "this" was.

"Toby, it's no—"

"It *is*," I said. "It *is* a big deal. What did he do? Don't tell me. I'm going to murder the guy. No, better yet, Wheedle's got a soft spot."

"The one on his head," she said.

"No, his Harley. I'm going to tear it apart limb by limb."

"Motorcycles don't have limbs."

"Shut up," I said. "This is serious. Where can I find a machine gun?"

Carolina was enjoying my anger far too much. She was trying to mask her titters. I didn't find it funny.

"A machine gun?" Giggles started falling out of her mouth.

"Okay, okay, a machine gun's probably too much, but…. *What?*"

Her giggles were turning into chortles.

"Okay, just tell me what he did. What did he do? Did you like it? Do you like him? Do you want him? Oh my

God, you want him, don't you? You are disgusting, Carolina. What?"

Her laughter burst out of her with a shriek.

"The things you make up in your head," she said, holding her sides in pain. "The creep just comes around the Texaco to buy cigarettes and says things like...." She started mimicking his high man-voice, "'Hey jailbait, how about you help me with my pump.' Or, 'How'd you like me to fill your tank, baby.' The kind of things that guys with little penises say."

A lawman. A Christian man. A Lutheran. It was disgusting, really, and such easy puns. Real amateur stuff.

We popped a bowl of popcorn and stayed awake a long time, the two of us, talking, pondering his incredibly small mind and discussing brain/genitalia ratios.

Over the next couple of days, I thought about how mad I was about Wheedle. How blood-in-my-eyes angry.

The thought of anyone, anywhere touching her filled me with jealousy and overflowed like a bad pour of hot coffee.

. . . . .

I was sitting on an old iron bench outside of The Precinct taking a break. It was late July, and the sun was bearing down, heating up the concrete and making wiggly waves on the asphalt road. I was flipping one of my flip-flops with my toes, watching the giant-sized red barrel of a cement truck across the way turning and turning the wet stuff as it poured down the chute. Men were standing with shovels and wheelbarrows, mixing and scraping the gunk to be poured for the sidewalks and parking lots that would replace the woods.

I had a stick in my hand, for some reason, tracing the name "Dickie" that was finger-written in an old square of sidewalk out front of The Precinct. "Dickie" was carved there way back when by none other than Officer Richard P. Wheedle when he was still officially a child.

I could see the passion of his self-centeredness, the deep capital "D," the "i'" meticulously dotted, the firm erection of the arm on the "k," the ego in the "e." But it was the "c" that always got me. The "c" was carved so deep and wide, with just enough curve in it to catch a child by the toe. To catch this child by the toe. I had forever stubbed my big toe in the "c" of Dickie's name.

I thought of Officer Wheedle as a boy, most likely blush-cheeked and chubby, pumped so full of the hot air of himself, he'd rise above all others. I thought of his need to have his name carved in concrete, a permanent reminder to all that he existed, which is consistent with my grave-marker theory.

I've been to the cemetery a lot lately. It's quiet, like the old beach. And it's nice, as far as graveyards go. When I'm there, I see names and dates and sometimes ceramic-mounted photos of the deceased on their headstones. All as if to say, "I was here! He was here! She was here!"

Yeah, I know that graves are a place for the living, too. I mean to visit and remember. But many graves are overgrown, so people either forgot to remember, or are too busy to remember, or moved away, or died themselves. Grave after grave sits still and silent for people like me, a stranger to the dead, to play names back in her head or say them out loud. To look at the dates and think about who they might have been.

One day, I was standing in front of Mitch's grave.

MITCHELL RUSSELL RENFREW
BELOVED SON
BORN 1952
DIED IN LOYAL SERVICE TO HIS COUNTRY
A SOLDIER IN VIETNAM

There was so much more to Mitch than all of that, so I sat right down with my notebook and started writing. When I was finished, I had written sixteen pages about Mitch. I didn't have any tape or anything, so I found an old Coke bottle and wound the whole bunch of those sheets up and stuck them in. I had to break the neck off to do it.

I put the thing next to his headstone. I thought about looking into one of those engravers and writing on the back and the sides of his headstone, so that someday, when no one who knew him is left alive, someone like me could really understand that a person as cool as Mitch did live.

But, back to my grave-marker theory. I think people want to last longer than their bodies do. They want to be remembered. They want to feel that they were important, so they carve their name in stone to prove they did exist.

Every day, I am reminded of the fact that Officer Wheedle indeed exists by the perch of his big butt on a vinyl-covered stool in The Precinct. I was thinking that all the reminder I would ever need was the tightly wrapped flesh of his being.

That thought inspired me to get up from my bench and walk into The Precinct. I found myself a milkshake tin and a large serving spoon, crossed Erie Street, passed by Zeke gossiping with the guys, and before they even knew I was there, I had filled my tin with wet cement and was back in front of The Precinct.

I took my spoon and artfully smeared the wet rock into every curve and dot and line of "Dickie," spending extra effort on the "c." No more stubbed toe. No more "Dickie."

Officer Wheedle's gonna have to die in order to have his name carved in stone. Hah! I thought. But it didn't make me feel any better.

As a matter of fact, that night, I had this dream that Carolina was riding on the back of Officer Wheedle's motorcycle, arms around his waist, holding on tight. Then, while his Harley was going full speed, she climbed up front and was straddling him, legs wrapped around his middle. She had her hands on the handlebars, steering without looking. His hands were all over the map.

I woke up and smacked her.

"Hey." The word out of her mouth for so rude an awakening. "What the hell?"

"I had a bad dream, sorry," I mumbled. But I was as ticked as if it were real. I rolled around in bed, pulling on covers, rearranging my pillow about a thousand times, huffing and puffing and sighing. Carolina threw her legs up off the side of the bed, stood all crushed up from sleeping, and with hands on her hips, yelled, "What's with you?"

She really liked her sleep.

"I'm ticked at you," I said.

"Why?"

"I had a dream that you and Officer Wheedle were practically doing…it…on his Harley."

"You are off your cracker," she moaned.

"It was so real," I groaned, putting my pillow over my head.

She jumped on top of the pillow and held it tight. I thought for sure she was going to let me die right then and there.

"Feels shitty, doesn't it?" she said as she let me up.

I grabbed some air and groaned again.

"God, Toby, you're too much," she said. "You can't go slapping at me for something you dreamed up."

I got up and went to the window, my back toward her. "I'm just weirding out, you know? I'm so scared that you're gonna leave me."

"For Officer Wheedle? You're nuts," she said.

"Oh, Lord. I don't know what's wrong. I just have this feeling I'm going to lose you…and…." I looked at her and took a big breath. "I'm sorry, Carolina, I really am. Sometimes I—I've got this hole in me," I tried to explain. "This feeling I'm going to lose…. It's so big. Don't you ever feel that way?"

She thought for a while. "I don't think I feel that way Tobe. It's kind of the opposite, like I don't want to be trapped."

"I want you to stay with me forever, and you don't want to be trapped."

We looked at each other, and for some reason, we started laughing.

fifteen

Muggy as Hell

July melted into an August morning to find me up and making donuts. Forget that it was a thousand degrees at six a.m. and as muggy as Hell. Well, maybe not Hell, since Hell (the popular version of it, anyway) doesn't have water, which means no humidity. So what I'm saying is, if Hell were situated on the edge of Lake Erie—and I'm not saying it's not—it would be as hot and humid as it was that day. Yes, I was sweating up a storm, just rolling the dough, and it occurred to me, at that moment, I was actually feeling happy. No kidding. Making donuts in the blazing kitchen in the early morning hours, when normal people are sleeping, sweat pouring out of me so I smell a little woodsy even after my shower. I'm there with the dough, a million percent humidity, that hot breeze blowing off the lake like a blast furnace through the screen, moving my sweat around, the sound of the oil bubbling in the fryer, the smell of coffee. Kasper at his dough, Dad at the window, staring, steaming cup in hand. And me, happy.

No radio that morning. No morning news is good morning news, if you ask me. All was quiet on the Eastern Front. I could hear only the sift of the leaves as the real storm was brewing out over the lake. The wind and the heat and the smells of the kitchen, that first light of the morning coming up, my body hot and alive, my hands doing the work they know by heart. I felt happy. No headlines. I just note it here, it being so rare and all.

I took my dough to the fridge to cool, walked over to my dad, and stood quietly, looking where he was looking—toward the lake, so I thought. The trees were swinging now, the branches of a willow practically horizontal.

"Wow, this'll be a good one," I said, feeling happy enough to make weather conversation.

"She left on a day like this, you know," he said, low, after a gap of silence.

She left? I thought, a little lost for a moment before I knew that he meant, *she* left. Well, after a lifetime of silence on the subject of *her* his reference seemed to blow in from nowhere.

I froze.

"A day just like this. Just up and left. Car pulled up, she walked out the door, got in, and was gone. Not a goddamned word."

My eyes started stinging; I wasn't sure why. Maybe I was thinking of me, in rubber pants, with a mother who could just leave without a goddamned word.

"I went to the window to look out. I didn't know what was going on. I saw that Chevy hightailing down the road. And not one goddamned...."

The silence that followed was crashing in my ears, and when I finally spoke, I felt like I was yelling from the bottom of a pit.

"I know what you felt like."

"Huh?" his brow asked.

"You haven't told me a goddamned word about her."

Pause.

"She left ya. She left me alone to raise the two of you kids."

"What was she like? Why did she leave?" My ears were still crashing.

He looked at me as if I were murmuring a foreign language. His eyes were saying "no comprendo."

"I want to know about my mother."

"She's dead."

"She's dead? Really dead? How? When? She's dead?"

"She's just dead," he said. "To me. To you. She never existed."

Now that the sealed tomb was open, I had to see all that was inside. I stepped in.

"I came from somewhere, from someone. She did exist. I want to know. You have no right—"

"I protected you from her. The less you know, the better." He snapped out the words.

"You protected me? From what? Nothing can be worse than not knowing."

"I wonder," he said, slowly regaining his usual casualness. He stared out the window again and silence stood guarding his back, arms folded like Mr. Clean.

"Dad."

"That's enough for now, Bee," he said. And I knew that would be all. I knew to back off. The harder you push the man, the further out he swims. Most of the time, he lives somewhere else, some island out there. I call it I'm-a-Failure Island. Can't be a cop, can't keep a wife, Whoa-is-Me Island. I was unsympathetic and angry, so I didn't back off this time. I knew it would get me nowhere, but I had to go on.

"I want to know about my mother." My words hung in large black letters in the thick air.

He turned and repeated his previous statement, in type that was louder, larger, and blacker than my own. "THAT'S ENOUGH FOR NOW, NOT ANOTHER WORD."

I walked out the door, preferring the weather outside to the atmosphere in there. It looked like a good day to take off.

Maybe that's what my mother thought.

Carolina was working a double shift at the Texaco, which left me with a prime opportunity to get some one on one on one with Me and Em and Em. I had to see 'em. I wanted facts. Whowhatwherewhenwhyhow? My brain was retrieving all I had learned in high school journalism. I felt mad and sad and mixed up, and all those feelings decided to have a meeting in my right foot as I made my way down the freeway. I'm sure the trooper would have pulled me over if that guy in the El Camino hadn't been more insane than I was.

When I got to the Aunts' they greeted me with Jell-O arms wide open and Emily said, "Honey, what?" And I just started crying and crying and crying. Sobbing, even. Me, of all people. I never did that, and now it seems like all I do. I was bawling my retinas out, nose running, face all red, spit stretching between my lips, throat all phlegmy, the works. Me. What the hell?

Emaline hugged me while Emily put on the tea. There was something good about the smell of their old place, all the wood scrubbed down, worn out, soft. There were cats, books, periodicals, stacks of albums, and a calm steadiness. When I heard the whistle of the kettle, I knew I was okay.

I blew my nose as Emily brought in tea and bologna sandwiches. "Bologna and ketchup?" She handed me a sandwich. On Wonder Bread. She knew my favorite breakfast. Emaline sat up and poured me a cup of tea. I watched the steam rise in a pin curl above it. She added milk and sugar, knowing already how I like to drink it.

All tomato-eyed and sobby, I told the Ems that I was turning into a wimp or something. They just sat back, sipping and chewing and waiting patiently for me to continue, like all the time in the world was to be had, like all their time was mine, like the three of us could sit there until the globe fell off its axis and smacked like a cue ball into the other eight planets. Emily rocked, stroking a cat. Emaline poured herself a second cup of tea. The grandmother clock chimed the passing minutes, and still all was silent. No word was spoken until my own.

"Who was my mother? Where did she go? What's the damn mystery?" I trailed off, lost in their faces.

There was a silence. All I could hear was the groan of the house, the settling of old bones.

I'd just about had it up to my ears with silence.

"Somebody say *something!*" I pretty much screamed the words.

The cats jumped. The Ems jumped. I jumped. Then the words came. From tongues through teeth, they slid through the air to my ears, worked their way to my brain and were translated into meaning, into feeling, into thought, into understanding. Some understanding.

"Your mother was a bit of a runaround," Emily said.

"You mean she slept around a lot," I said.

"She was a beautiful woman," Emaline said.

"Oh, yes, beautiful," Emily said.

"She was blonde," Emaline said.

"That came out of a box," said Emily.

"Oh, yes, definitely," said Emaline.

Their conversation volleyed back and forth like a tennis match. I wanted some real information, but even her boxed hair color was news, so I wanted to hear it all.

"Men liked Laura," Emily said.

Laura—it was odd to hear my mother's name.

"She had quite the figure," Emily said. "Men buzzed around her like bees to a rose."

"Like hummingbirds to nectar," said Emaline. "They pounced like cats on catnip."

Emily gave Emaline a dark look. Emaline took a drink of tea to shut herself up.

"She had a weakness," Emily said.

I was weak myself from crying and tired from a lifetime of waiting, but I almost felt like giggling.

"It's one of those things that's hard to see at first," Emaline said.

"Well, some of us saw it," Emily said. "But Emil was so head-over-heels happy, some thought he couldn't see it."

Emil and Laura Renfrew. I tried to imagine them— two young people in a donut shop.

"Because he was *too much* in love," Emaline added.

"And oh, how people talked," Emily said.

"They thought your father was blind as a bat and dumb as an ox," Emaline said. She liked her idioms.

"But we knew him since he was born," Emily said.

"The cutest little thing," Emaline said. "And that tiny pecker."

Emily gave Emaline a darker look.

"Oh, dear, that was inappropriate. It's just that he was such a minikin."

Emily cleared her throat and went on, "But when he was a young adult—"

"Twenty or so," Emaline interrupted.

"Twenty-two or -four," Emily said.

"Give or take," Emaline said. "Or maybe he was eighteen."

"No, he was definitely older than eighteen," Emily said.

"It's so hard to remember," Emaline said.

Okay, so watching them was more like watching a superball bouncing rapidly between two walls.

"He caught the mumps," Emily said.

"A bad case," Emaline said. "The worst."

"Your Grandma Pearl," Emily said.

"God rest her and bless her," Emaline said.

"Pearl told us that the doctors told Emil that he was most likely sterile," Emily said. "So when Laura was pregnant…."

"He likely knew," Emaline said. "Or at least suspected."

"Your father's no idiot," Emily said.

"But he loved that woman," Emaline said. "We knew him since he was born."

"He loved her," Emily said. "And he loves you kids, both of you."

"So, both Friday and I…." I choked. They both sat back to listen. My words hung in the air all by themselves for a while. Not only did I not know my mother, now I maybe had a father I knew nothing about. This was heavy stuff.

"So, I'm a bastard?"

"No, no, no, no. Laura did fess up about Friday," Emily said. "But you…."

"You are just a miracle," Emaline said.

"A miracle," Emily underlined the statement. "You're too much like him not to be blood."

"The spitting image," Emaline said.

"More of a combination," Emily said.

"But nobody's sure, since my mother was a slut," I said.

"Now that's harsh," Emily said.

"She had a weakness," Emaline said.

"Why didn't anybody tell me?"

"It's a lot for a child to understand," Emily said.

"But you're an adult now," Emaline added.

If that was true, why did I suddenly feel like a baby?

. . . . .

I called Carolina at the Texaco, and when her shifts were over, Friday drove her to the Ems'. She and I stayed a couple days. I ate a lot of bologna and drank a lot of tea. I told my dad where I was. I didn't want to be rude, just away.

Friday just hung out that night. He knew a little more than I did a little sooner. If it bothered him, he didn't show it so much. I suppose to him the past was not as important as the present. After all, Anna was what really mattered to my brother.

Although it was good to be with the Ems—it's nice to be spoiled and doted on, for sure—a couple days was quite enough. I got up early on the third day and dressed to leave for work. I woke Carolina, who was a little crabby about it. She really wasn't a morning person. The

Ems were up, and I gave them big, grateful hugs goodbye. Carolina drank about a gallon of coffee.

"Too much caffeine is not good for you, dear," Emaline said.

"It can raise your blood pressure," Emily said.

"And aggravate your rheumatism," Emaline added.

"She's too young for rheumatism," Emily said.

"Well, caffeine could bring an early onset," Emaline said.

Yes, it was time to go.

I drove my little beater of a Mustang home to The Precinct, where it was business as usual. Um, kind of.

S u c h   A r e   B o o b s

I had no sooner walked into the door and put on my apron, a little nervous about how things might go, when Min came busting in, fresh from a two-week vacation. The key syllable there was "bust." Min had doubled her cup size—bra-wise I'm talking—and there she was, tightly tucked into her uniform.

"Well, have a good, uh, vacation?" Friday asked, in a stunned politeness.

Min put her hands on her rump, pushed her chest out, and replied, "Why, yes I did, Friday. Thank you for asking."

"Do anything…interesting?" Kasper asked.

"Well, I got myself a boob job." She sparkled.

"Really?" I asked.

Her eyes became as big as Orphan Annie's. "What? Are you blind? Look at these titties, firm and fit, like a sixteen-year-old's. And they'll never sag. They're those new siliconie thingies. Just a little something to spice up the love life."

Friday hooted.

Kasper commented that his love life could use a charge, and maybe he should get a pair for his coffee table. My dad didn't say much of anything at the time, although later I heard him say, "Damn pert" to Kasper in the kitchen. Kasper then said something about the whole thing being beyond his apprehension.

That Min.... I always knew she had a crack in her saucer, but this took the cake. Instaboobs. Why? Her other boobs seemed fine to me, caved-in bra and all.

"What do they feel like?" I asked her when we were alone.

"Come'ere." She took my hand, pulled me into the john, and closed the door. She opened her blouse a bit. "Go ahead, feel."

"I meant, what do they feel like from the inside," I said, not wanting to feel the part of Min that should have remained in her blouse. "Do they...you...hurt?"

"A little, but it's worth it, Kid. The scars will go away. Go ahead, feel. I know you're not shy about such things."

"I'm not going to feel your boobs," I said.

"I'm not asking you to feel me up," she said, sounding hurt. "I thought you were just curious, that's all." She buttoned up her blouse.

"I was, I am, can I?" I asked, feeling obligated in a weird way. It was still awfully early in the morning for all of this.

She smiled and I poked the side of her left breast quickly.

"It feels rubbery," I observed.

"Firmness—that's what you feel. Firmness and youth through the miracle of plastic surgery," she said, sounding like a brochure.

I pondered the thought of youthful boobs on a not-so-youthful body. "Oh," I said. Then took a moment to play back her words: *you're not shy about such things.* But I let them go. I walked from that weird scene smack into another going on at the donut counter as I picked up the coffee pot to pour refills for the early-bird customers.

"Faggots are the scum and scourge of the earth," Officer Wheedle pontificated with his mouth full, jelly dripping down his chin. As I stood in front of him my eyes became telephoto and I could see the grease of his sweat, the stubble of his razor rash, the sticky jelly, and the chewed-up food in his teeth clearly. I became nauseated. He wiped his chin and continued, still chewing.

"That Anita Bryant, now there's a girl to be praised," Officer Wheedle spouted. Anita Bryant was a beauty queen turned singer turned orange juice spokesperson who loudly protested against gay rights.

"Yeah, that Anita, she knows what's up. What's right is right and what's wrong is wrong. I agree with her," Wheedle said, closing somebody else's *Time* magazine. "She believes, that God—and I am 100 percent with God on this—does not like homos because homos eat each other's sperm—ugh—and since sperm is used to create babies, they are eating life. Disgusting. Those sickos should be hung."

I bet you wish you were, you piss-poor innuendo-blabbing, tiny-pistol-toting sad excuse for a lawman, I thought. Then I heard Min mumble just before she said out loud, "I guess poor old Anita's husband never got a BJ from that girl of his."

Officer Wheedle spewed all he'd chewed on the front of me.

Everybody stopped what they were doing. I looked down at my shirt.

"Gee-zus, Wheedle, now I'm going to have to disinfect my clothes."

"Take the Fels-Naptha to the mouth of that waitress friend of yours while you're at it. Renfrew!" I don't know why he thought he needed to yell for my dad, he was standing right there. A little latent tattling I guess.

My dad looked attentively at Officer Wheedle, trying hard not to laugh. Kasper was snickering. The poor lawman didn't know what to do with himself. He put on his hat and stomped out.

"I'm going to have to burn this shirt," I said as I went upstairs to change.

"He started it," I heard Min say. "He's the one who said sperm."

It wasn't until I was halfway up the stairs that it occurred to me that Officer Wheedle was talking about me. I didn't really think of myself as a homosexual, as part of a group of undesirables to be rallied against by the orange juice lady. I was a girl with a girlfriend. I loved someone of the same gender. Sure, I struggled with it from time to time inside myself, but I didn't think much about how people in general would react. Just my dad. I guess old Wheedle had given me some food for thought. I just hoped it wouldn't leave a permanent stain.

That event collided headfirst with the news that Elvis had died. For some reason his death brought people swarming through our doors. It was within minutes, or hours, I don't know. The shop was hopping. Everybody was wailing about how the King was dead. People were saying that everyone would remember where they were when they heard the news, the same as how nobody would forget what they were doing when they heard JFK was assassinated.

The real talk about Elvis came days later, when it was further revealed that Elvis had died on the toilet. Most of the men could understand and sympathize with the situation. "I've laid some killer turds in my day," one of them started. And then it went on and on and on. You've heard of big fish stories. Well, these were far worse, more unbelievable, and all told over donuts and coffee.

Men and toilets; they're a weird pairing. I can't tell you how many times I've seen my dad and brother arm themselves with reading material, then head for the john. Our male customers do it all the time—pick up the paper, fold it under their arms, and excuse themselves for fifteen or twenty minutes. In *our* restroom. They camp there. I don't get it. Then again, I'm not sure I'm meant to…or want to.

I think it's the day after Elvis died that I remember most. Things were slower, and I was sitting at a booth, watching the apartments go up. The pounding gave me a headache and a sense of helplessness. A good chunk of the woods was gone, and these skeletons were being built. I could see the layouts, small, depressing cubes of living space. I was sighing into my coffee when my dad seated himself across from me. He had something in his hand.

"I was thinking about what you said, Bee," he began. "And I shouldn't have kept this from you." He handed me an old color photo of a young woman holding a little baby girl. They were both dressed up, like it was a special day. The baby had her head on the woman's shoulder, shy, hand curled up, holding a piece of donut. The woman's eyes were staring somewhere past the camera. There was a cooped-up smile on her lips. But there we were. Finally. Me and my mother. My eyes couldn't take in enough. I was tearing up, staring. I couldn't speak.

"Your momma…" my dad continued, looking at his hands. "She had this way about her. She made me feel so tall, so strong." He looked at me. "But she liked lots of men, Toby. A wedding band meant nothing to her. The guy she left with, well, he was just one in a whole string. I didn't know, at least, I wouldn't let myself know it, until she was gone."

"So, I put two and two together later." He choked a little. "We got married fast, and Friday did come a little soon. I thought I just got lucky. And you.…"

I'd heard all of this and more that day at the Ems's, but tears still dripped down my nose.

"And you. I could have had blood tests, but as far as I was—I am—concerned, you are—both of you are—my flesh and my blood. But she, she just left you."

My dad's eyes were wet.

"She came back once, and when I saw her, my first thought was, 'She's not taking those babies.' But all she wanted was my John Hancock on divorce papers. She didn't even ask about you."

I could have lived my whole life without hearing that last sentence.

I felt sad as I studied this woman's face. My dad studied me. I expected him to be true to his MO and walk away because his emotions were strong, but he didn't. He sat with me and took my hand.

"You're my girl, Bee."

I looked down at the photo again. My mother looked exactly nothing like Suzanne Pleshette.

seventeen

Sinkers

After the days of numbing talk of Min's boob job, Officer Wheedle's spew, the hype over Elvis, and the news that my father may or may not be my father and that my brother Friday is really my half-brother, I felt I needed a little quiet. I took myself to my rock on the beach.

I was listening to the silence between the waves licking the sand and the gulls searching for fish. I smelled the air and felt the breeze and bits of lake water on my skin.

My rock. My place.

I held the photo of my mother and me in my hand.

In the corner of my ear, I heard a soft, "Hey." It was Friday. "Come on," he said as he walked toward the edge of the lake, head down, a posture I'd seen him take for as long as I could remember. He was looking for skippers.

Since he was a kid, Friday could skip stones across the surface of Erie better than anyone around. It was his birthday tradition, one he started himself, to make the rock skip once for each year of his life. He'd practice all year. It was almost impossible to count the skips after a dozen or so, his technique required speed, but he knew how many skips the stone made. And since Friday was an honest guy who was hard on himself, when he told you the number, you could believe him.

I had wanted to skip like Friday, but my stones would sink like, well, stones. So Friday helped me create my own tradition. On my birthday, I'd sink my sorrows. I'd take a rock and throw away anything bad that happened during that year. That way, he said, I'd be ready for new good things.

I got off my rock, walked to the water's edge, and stood next to him. My muscles ached like I had the flu.

"Can I see the picture?" he asked.

I handed him the photo. He looked at it hard for a few minutes, then handed it back to me. He tossed a stone up and down in the palm of his hand as if weighing it before slinging it across the water.

"She came to see us once," he said.

"What are you talking about?"

"I was nine, I think. It was my birthday. Yeah, I know I was nine, I remember. I brought you down here because I wanted to do nine skips. I'd been practicing. Dad told me we couldn't go down to the water. It was getting dark. I could take you to play on the swings on the bluff, but not by the water. But I wanted to skip. I was looking for stones while keeping my eye on you. You were doing your helicopter thing."

I liked to twirl like a helicopter when I was a kid—the kind that fall from maple trees, not the other kind. I'd hold one arm out and twirl until I fell, and then do it again. And again. I kind of miss doing that. I miss a lot of things these days.

Friday went on. "I remember looking at you twirling, and then I got caught up finding the perfect stone. I always want the perfect stone. I looked up again and you were gone, like that. I couldn't see you for a minute and I panicked.

"Finally, I saw you. The sun was going down, but I saw you walking away from me down the beach, holding the hand of some adult. I freaked out and started running.

"When I caught up, I saw that you were with a woman. She looked familiar, Toby. She said my name. It was her. I was scared—we weren't supposed to be on the beach. She said my name. I just grabbed you and pulled you away. When I looked back, she was just staring at us. Her hair was blowing and her clothes were blowing and the sun was sinking. It was November. It was cold. It was my birthday.

"I walked away from her. I took us away from her."

I looked at my brother. He had pain in his eyes, in his face. I couldn't say anything. I bent over and picked up a large sinking stone. I threw it hard.

Plonk.

"I think I remember that, Friday. It's fuzzy. But I kind of do."

"I walked away from her, Toby. It's been years, and I still think of her every day."

I bent over and found another sinker. I handed it to my brother. He looked at me, then turned and heaved it into the water.

Thunk. Plonk. It hit a big rock and then hit the water. That one felt good.

We heaved and threw and thunked and plonked until our arms were sore and our legs were sore and we couldn't do it anymore.

Then, my brother and I walked home in silence to make our supper.

eighteen

My Wildest Dreams

They say things happen in threes. Well, that's what happened to me when it came to dreams. Dream number one was about Officer Wheedle, which I already mentioned. The second dream found me walking over some crusty land, my feet sinking down with each step. Like I was walking through deep snow, only there was no snow. I realized that I wasn't walking over land—I was walking over the surface of a donut. A buttermilk cake donut. Crusty, crunchy almost. With each step, my foot would sink into the cake below.

I kept walking. For a while, there was nothing around me but the deep-fried surface. But eventually, I saw this shaft of bright light shooting straight up, as if a searchlight had been buried and aimed toward space. I trudged over to the light and saw it was coming from the hole in the donut. I leaned forward, I saw freedom shining up at me, all I had to do was throw myself forward. I knew that I should do it, but I was scared. I wanted to jump, but the light was blinding and I became dizzy. Fear overtook me and instead of moving toward the light, I threw myself back and my whole body sank into the donut. It swallowed me up. I thought I was dead at first, but then I could smell vanilla and cinnamon. I reached up, tore off a piece of donut, and put it in my mouth. It made my whole body feel warm and safe and good. In my dream, I slept long and deep.

In real life, I woke up. It was only midnight. How could all that donut walking happen in less than an hour? It took me a while to fall back to sleep. I started dreaming again.

In this dream, I was looking through an open sliding glass door, watching a jet fly across the bluest sky. Suddenly, the jet bent like a pointer pinkie, turning to purposely hit a big blackbird. The bird, which at first glance looked like a pair of dress trousers, came plummeting down toward me. I grabbed at the door, trying desperately to slide it shut, but no luck. That huge black bird hit me, smack in my heart.

This time, I woke up with my heart slamming. I needed an interpretation. Fast.

Carolina's analysis was simple. "It means you should go back to sleep and leave me alone." She put her pillow over her head and accused me of letting gas.

Later that day, I asked Min for an interpretation. She said that the plane was phallic, as in male genitalia, and the dress slacks turning into a blackbird symbolized death.

"I get how the blackbird might be death, but the trousers?" I asked.

"You get dressed up for a funeral, don't you?" she said, sounding logical.

"Um...."

She went on, voice sad. "The funeral makes sense." She paused, wiping her eyes, obviously thinking about Mitch. "But it could be something more. Phallic symbol plus men's slacks equals men. Blackbird equals death. Hitting your heart, the universal symbol of romantic love, means that your heart is dead to the male phallus/male romantic love, which only makes sense, Kid, does it not?"

"Uh," I replied, kind of sorry I asked.

But this dream discussion had suddenly opened up a whole new subject, and I decided to tiptoe in. "So, the Carolina and me cat's out of the bag?"

She laughed. "Kid, you were never in the bag. I kept testing, but you wouldn't budge. And you are always okay by me."

"Does my dad know?" I asked.

"You should talk to your father about that," she answered, sounding strangely motherly.

"Uh, right. Thanks, Min," I said. Her words felt good. I immediately put talking to my dad about Carolina on my mental backburner—way in back. My dream still was not explained to my satisfaction.

I went to the next viable interpreter.

I had been dropping by Auntie Flo's house at least once a week since Mitch asked me to start the Camaro. I had stepped it up to twice a week since Mitch's funeral.

She was doing alright. As alright as could be expected.

"It's a warning from the Almighty!" Auntie Flo cried, on hearing my dream.

"God's warning me?" I asked.

"Not you, me!" She practically ran to the fridge to get herself a Miller.

"My dream's a warning to you?" I didn't get it. "Wouldn't *my* dream be about *me*?"

"Oh, your dream. You just had bad gas," she said. "I'm talking about the dream I had two nights ago. I believe it was a vision sent from God Almighty as a warning to me."

So now the conversation was about her. Oh, well.

"I was in my bed," she began, popping open the beer and taking a swig straight from the can, unsalted. Now that Mitch was officially dead, she dropped her excuses for drinking. "My very bed...the marital bed I share with your Uncle Nick, only I woke and Nick was nowhere to be seen. I was alone—or so I thought. Then I saw the figure."

She took another slug from the can.

"Want me to get you a glass? Salt?" I asked, concerned about her behavior. She shook her head to indicate that I'd just better sit still and listen. I did.

"It was the Devil." She took another gulp. "Satan himself was standing over me, as real to me as you are now. He was ugly and warty. His breath was hot and smelled of old cabbage. His fingers were crooked and pointy. I could even see his fingernails, which I knew had never seen a manicure in eternity. It was the Devil, clear as day it was."

"Wow." I was riveted.

"He leaned over me, right over my bed, dripping the almighty-knows-what over my clean coverlet. He pointed to the door and told me I had five minutes to get out. Five minutes."

"So, what did you do?" I asked, excited.

"Well, I tried to kick off the covers, but at first those blankets felt like they were sewn with lead. Then they were so light they floated up above me, like a summer cloud. I slipped right off the mattress and headed for the door. But, out of the corner of my eye, what did I see?"

"What? What?" I couldn't wait.

"My Humbly figurine. The little mailman your Uncle Nick bought me when we were first dating. The collectible. I thought, 'Well, I've got five minutes and the door is right there. Surely I have time to get my Humbly figurine.' And I went and grabbed that sweet little statuette off my dresser.

"Just then, my eyes came to rest on that genuine silver-plated hand mirror that my mamma—rest her and bless her—had left to me upon her passing, and I decided to take that, too. Then I thought of my fox collar, you know how I adore that collar. I went to the closet and took it. And I went on like that—I was picking things up left and right, up and under. My arms were laden when I remembered the time."

"What happened, Auntie?" This was too good.

"Well, I dropped everything and ran for the door."

"And…."

"Glory," she said, sucking her beer can dry, "Satan stretched his crooked, horny self—I mean literally horny, you know, like a rhinoceros has—across that doorway and said, 'Too late.' Then I woke up."

"Auntie Flo," I squealed like a girl, not knowing I could squeal like a girl, "that's what I call a dream."

"It is not a dream," she said sternly. "I will say it again, it was a vision—a message straight from the good Lord above."

"What is the message?" I asked.

"I must give up all of my worldly possessions!" she said, almost exasperated. "I must rid myself of these things and come to him. The Devil will have me, otherwise. And I will never see my own beloved son again."

I thought that was so sad. Besides, Auntie Flo loved her things, and believe me, she had a lot to love. Among the golden ivy and velvet, reflecting in the gold-veined mirrors, were her earthly treasures. Every shelf, every drawer, every closet, every bit of drywall, every cupboard, every nook and cranny of every nook and cranny was covered with crap, stuffed with stuff. In my head (and only in my head) I referred to my dear Auntie Flo as Queen Plethora. When it came to shopping, she reigned supreme. Rummage ran like blue blood through her veins.

"Auntie Flo, you can't get rid of all your stuff," I said, knowing that she couldn't, and trying to mentally tally the number of dumpsters it would take.

"The good Lord has spoken to me. I must abide," she said in her best Baptist tongue.

"It was just a dream," I said.

"A vision," she corrected. "I must flush myself."

"Flush yourself…okay," I said. "Can I have this, then?" I waved a fringed-sateen *Souvenir of Niagara Falls* pillow.

"Take it, please. Save me from myself," she said, waving me out the door. "I must begin my purge."

I left with my new pillow under my arm and something to nibble on—dreams and the subconscious.

My high school psychology course introduced me to the notion of the subconscious. My teacher was more interested in telling stories of his wasted youth than teaching, but he did manage to spew out a few terms like id, ego, and superego. And though I'd be hard-pressed to tell you exactly what those terms mean, the notion of the subconscious, a place inside our own selves that we don't know much about, was and remains very interesting to me. My theory, which I probably stole, is that we know a whole lot more than we think we know, and if we knew how to listen to ourselves, we'd know more about what we think we don't know or don't have any idea that we do know.

Sometimes I just sit on my rock, looking out at Erie and trying to listen to my subself, but I usually get distracted. One day, I was looking at the lake, which I always thought was rather desperate with those waves that keep grabbing at the shore and slipping away. Grabbing and slipping away. Grabbing and slipping. I've always looked at the lake as trying to hold onto the shore and not being able to get a grip.

But it occurred to me this one day that the lake isn't desperate at all. The lake is deliberate. The beach disappeared over my lifetime, and it was the lake that took it, one wave at a time. I sat on my rock and watched the very clever lake and started thinking about what else has disappeared in my lifetime. The woods that were always there until they were bulldozed and chain sawed away almost overnight. Then I thought of the people who disappeared, which made me feel sad and not want to think anymore. And besides, what I was supposed to be doing at the time was making a Rubberware run for The Precinct.

So, I got into my old Mustang and drove to the Bargain Barn. I was taking the long way to the Containers, Bins & Misc. Storage Items when I saw Auntie Flo strolling down aisle seven. It was a couple of weeks after she told me about her dream, and there she was, eyes blazing like a blue-light special, another cartful away from her God. I looked right at her, but she didn't see me, her vision being obstructed.

Seeing her made me feel even sadder for her, so I went back to The Precinct Rubberware-less. My dad didn't understand, and I didn't know how to explain, so he threw up his hands in frustration, which made me feel even worse.

I didn't have any dreams that night. I felt as if the big blackbird had built a nest on my heart and had no plans to migrate. I held myself tight to Carolina, and for the first time, I think, it wasn't a forever tight. It was more of a grateful-I-had-her-that-night tight. As the early grey of morning lit the edges of my bedroom shade, I kissed her between her shoulder blades, squeezed the tears back into my eyes, and got up to dress for work.

n i n e t e e n

P o l i c e   D r a m a

There were plenty of cop shows on television. *Dragnet*, which followed the adventures of Friday's namesake, Sergeant Joe Friday; my personal childhood favorite, *The Mod Squad*; and the now sadly gone *Adam-12*. But nothing on TV quite matched the police drama that played itself out in the real world once Officer Wheedle figured out that Carolina and I were more than just friends.

I'm not sure where or how it occurred to Officer Chubby Cheeks. Maybe when his innuendos turned into physical advances and Carolina blew him off. Wait, not the best choice of words—when Carolina told him to back off. I just know when I started feeling his hot eyeballs burning into my skin at the shop. He spent a couple days staring at me before he came out with it.

Friday was behind the counter, playing donut jerk—filling bags and boxes with donuts to go. My dad was standing in a corner, jawing with Mr. Salida from the 40 Winks. Kasper was in the kitchen, which must have also completely swallowed Min, because I alone was left to hustle the coffee pot around for at least fifteen minutes.

I had just returned from Booth #2, where Mr. Beeman from Beeman Drugs was deep in conversation with Joe Parman from Parman's Dry Goods. I remember thinking, for the millionth time, what is a dry good anyway? Crusty Jones, the singing barber—dubbed so by Friday because he used to hum in his ear while he cut his hair—was standing next to Beeman and Parman's booth, gesticulating. Their conversation seemed to be political in nature, so I poured quickly and ducked away with the words "well, that's what you get when you have a peanut farmer for a president" trailing in my ears.

Officer Wheedle was perched on his stool, badge all shiny, belly lopping over his belt. It was about time for him to take off for his appointed rounds, but he appeared to be parked there with no sign of movement. I looked at the clock as I approached the counter.

"Your meter's about to run out, Officer Wheedle," I said.

"Listen." He hissed out the "s," and his face looked angry. I was taken by surprise and stood silent, coffee pot in my hand. "I know what you are up to, and it ain't right."

I don't know why he used the word "ain't," exactly. Maybe he was making some kind of cop point.

"What—"

"Don't 'what' me, girl," his voice rasped from his throat.

Girl?

"You and jailbait better watch yourselves, because the law is going to be watching you," he whispered.

He picked his hat up off the counter, got off his stool, and hitched up his pants.

"I'll be watching," he growled into my ear again. He put on his hat with emphasis, turned, and slammed through the door.

Uh, oh. I looked around. Beeman and Parman and the singing barber were all looking at me. Luckily, Salida and my dad were still lapping up each other's words. Friday was busy with a woman who wanted a box of squares.

I looked at the table of men and shrugged all nonchalant, as if to say, "What's gotten into him?" But inside, fear was bubbling up like oil in the deep fryer.

I'd never been a target of what seemed to be rage before. Not like that. Wheedle scared the coffee out of me. I had to go to the bathroom.

In the john, I looked at myself in the mirror. Toby Renfrew, Pubic Enemy Number One. Lesbo at Large. I tried to look dangerous. I did my best mugshot pose. Someone knocked on the door.

"Just a minute," I yelled.

Toby Renfrew, wanted for sexual miss-conduct.

Again, the knock. "Toby, we could use some help out here." It was Min.

Geezus. She disappeared into the kitchen, leaving me holding the pot, and I couldn't even take a few minutes in the can. I opened the door and looked out. The place was overrun.

An elderly woman shoved her way into the bathroom.

"What the hell, did someone bus these people in?"

Someone had. A busload of senior citizens en route to the Dayton Air Force Museum had stopped by for snacks. You would have thought someone could have left them in the bus and come in to buy a half-dozen variety boxes.

"We've always heard of this place, but have just never made it out here," a plump woman in white pedal pusher jeans and matching jacket that fit tightly over a navy-and-white striped shirt was telling my dad. She had him pinned near the front counter. Her white crinkle patent leather-like purse hung by a short strap in the crook of her arm. Her chubby feet were poured into little white shoes. She was kind of adorable.

"Do you have any t-shirts?" an old man was asking Min.

T-shirts?

"My grandson collects t-shirts from famous places, and he wanted me to pick one up."

Famous places? What the...?

They kept us busy for a good twenty minutes and about wiped us out. We all went back to the kitchen to fry up some more donuts. We always had an emergency stash of dough for occasions such as this.

"What did that guy say about t-shirts?" I asked. "He said something about this place being famous."

Min shook her head, indicating that she had no idea.

"Maybe it was that article," my dad said.

A reporter from the *Plain Dealer* had come by to do a feature story on the shop in the spring. We didn't think much about it, just framed it and hung it in the front with some of the other stories and reviews. Most were from smaller papers. Some were yellow old by now.

"Maybe we should make t-shirts," Friday said. "We'll make a little cartoon of the square donut or something. I know the guy who does the artwork for *The Buzzard*. Why don't I ask him to take a crack at it?"

The Buzzard was a handle for a big radio station.

"T-shirts." My dad was pondering the thought. "I like it."

That was the day we all began to realize that our little donut shop had gained a reputation as a classic in the greater Cleveland area.

Speaking of reputations—for the first time in my life, I had to start thinking about mine.

twenty

Lardass

I had planned to tell Carolina what Officer Blubber Butt had said when she returned from the Texaco. She surprised me by coming home early, and she seemed nervous and looked kind of pale.

"Are you okay?" I asked.

"Damned lardass," she said.

"Oh my God, he got to you, too?"

"What do you mean?" she asked.

"He was in here, threatening to narc on us."

"He just wants me, that's all," she said. "I told him to go to hell."

"Whoa, he still doing the innuendo thing?" I asked.

"Worse. I was in the back of the station by the lavs this afternoon, taking a smoke break. He pulled his patrol car up too close, pinning me in. He tried to get me into the car, but I wouldn't. He got real ticked then."

"What the…" I said.

"He got out of the car and came over and shoved his fat puss into my face. He said he'd done some checking and knew all about me. Nobody has anything on me, so I called him a liar."

"What did he do?"

"He grabbed my wrist, twisted it to show my scar and said he knew all about my institutionalization. He said I was a danger to myself and others, and he was going to build a case against me if I didn't cooperate."

"How?"

"Uh, Toby, I think you can take a guess."

"Shit," I said. "We've got to turn him in."

"Toby, he's threatening us. He wants to say that I'm some unstable nutcase that seduced you into a lesbian relationship. All he really wants is a blowjob."

I felt a sudden need to grow up. "Carolina, you didn't, did you?"

"Christ, Toby, what do you think I am? I'm not the feeble little mental patient he thinks I am. Let him make his threats."

I felt sick to my stomach.

"How would you feel if people knew? About us, I mean," she said.

I didn't know.

"They probably already do anyway, Toby. If nobody talks about it, they can pretend that they don't know so they can go about their business. If we are pegged as lesbians, people will feel forced to react, and it might not be pretty."

I didn't have any words.

"If I left, Toby, you wouldn't need to deal with all this right now."

I felt like I was in a nightmare.

"But you'd have to deal with yourself, sooner or later," she said.

I sat down, not able to take the whole thing in. It was like one minute everything was fine and the next, I was hit by a great big rock. Before I could recover or get out of the way, an avalanche was on top of me. My breath became short. Partially because, as big as Carolina talked, I could tell she was scared, too.

"Shit," was all I could think of saying.

"You got that right," she said.

I thought for a minute. "Everybody knows about the Ems and nobody says anything."

"Right, nobody says anything because nobody ever said anything. I told you, if people can pretend, they will. He wants to make a case out of this and make us look sick. He wants to make trouble. He wants to be the Anita Bryant of Ohio."

"I like being a lesbian," I said.

Carolina smiled.

"It's like nothing fit in my whole life, then everything fit. You did that for me."

"It was pretty obvious, Tobe."

"What was?"

"I knew you were a little dyke the minute I saw you."

"Wha…how?" I asked, feeling a little dumb.

"Um, the way you walk. The way you talk. The way you flirted with me."

"Flirted?"

"You *poured sugar* into my coffee," she said, laughing. "How many customers do you do that for?"

"Oh, yeah," I said, seeing her point. I started to giggle. "And then you, you *licked* your palm. I thought I was going to die."

She laughed again. "That was good, I'll admit it. You should have seen the look on your face. You did look like you were going to die. I wasn't planning on sticking around long, but you were really, really cute."

"I was?"

"Well, what do you think? Yes, you were cute. You *are* cute."

"Cute?"

"God, Toby. You're sexy-cute and funny. You have no idea how funny you are. You don't even try. Why do you think I stay?"

"I always think you're going to go. Sometimes you act like you're going to go at any second."

"I know, and you act like you expect me to go. We're a real pair."

"I wouldn't trade this for anything, Carolina, I really wouldn't. And I'm not going to let old kangaroo keester ruin things for us."

"I like that, Tobe. What's your plan? Want to come clean to your dad?"

"Well, uh…."

Carolina started laughing.

I sighed. "Is that what you think Wheedle's going to do—go to my dad?"

"I have no idea what rhino rump has up his sleeve."

"Bovine butt"

"Enorm-ass"

"Officer Plumpy."

We were both quiet for a minute.

"I don't want to lose this, Tobe. I don't want that fat bastard to take this away from me. I'm not going to let him."

I had never seen her face the way it looked at that moment. She scared me a little, and yet her words made me happy.

"What do you want to do?" we both asked at the same time.

"Uh," I said.

"Hummm," she said.

twenty-one

The Enlightened

Auntie Flo came into The Precinct, acting all nervous and funny.

I said, "What gives, Auntie Flo?" and she got all blushy. She hisses that she has to talk to me real serious and I get worried, like maybe she has "the big C" like her best friend Mildred or something, so I told my dad I had to go talk to Auntie Flo.

We took a walk down to the old beach, and she pulled a book out of her purse and handed it to me: *Sex Today: The Modern Guide*. She shoved the thing into my chest, and said she marked some pages for me to read. She burst into tears and scurried off. I was worried and upset. I didn't get it. I started after her, and she stopped, turned, and waved me away. Lord, I hate to be waved away.

I went to my rock and opened the parts she'd marked.

Female homosexuals.

Oh, Lord, Wheedle, strike three, I thought. I read on, kind of curious. *As with the male homosexual, lesbians do not have what it takes to round out the picture. Two vaginas, no penis, the girls simply strike out.*

I looked at this paperback's cover and read: *#1 Bestseller.* I turned to the back and saw a smiling man in a starched white shirt and read:

Dr. Martin Horn, MD, a Los Angeles therapist, has combined extensive research and the personal stories of his private patients to bring a fresh perspective, truth and enlightenment to sex, speaking freely about a subject often explained in hushed tones in dark places. A true sexual revolutionary, he writes with no personal morality injected. Dr. Horn broaches even the most intimate of subjects candidly, breaking through secrecy with insight, exchanging anxiety for assurance in this authoritative text.

I reopened the text and read on:

The female homosexuals kiss a lot compared to the male of their ilk. They fondle and hug trying to create a facsimile of love. The males usually want to cut straight to the orgasm then move on to the next fellow. Female "couples" may play at the "relationship" longer than the males, but frankly, they are all doomed. True love is an impossibility. Lasting relationships? No. Real fulfillment? Never.

The section on lesbians, I noted, was in the chapter called *The Oldest Profession,* not in the chapter on homosexuality, which was reserved for males only. Female homosexuals were not even equal to male homosexuals in this expert's view of things. I looked at the black and white photo of this man on the back cover, still smiling, holding a pipe in his hand, dress shirt open, without a tie. Expressing, perhaps, a less stodgy approach to things. There he was, posing for his book jacket, *breaking through secrecy with insight, exchanging anxiety for assurance.*

I turned to the section on male homosexuality, placed as it was between *Masturbation* and *Sado Masochism.*

A homosexual can change if he wants to, but must find a therapist with the skills to cure the disease. The good news is, he can go on to live a happy heterosexual life.

Auntie Flo had wandered into the same section and highlighted that one, then wrote a phone number of one Pastor Brown, from the Christ Almighty Baptist Church. I read more highlighted parts:

Homosexuals who keep house together have no chance at real love or happiness. They will have a life of envy, backbiting, discontent and lies. Cheating is a way of life. They seethe with hidden anger; breathe bitterness.

I read, again, the back jacket, *A true sexual revolutionary, he writes with no personal morality injected.*

I looked again at the peacock of a man in the publicity photo. I thought of my Auntie Flo's worried face. I thought of me. I turned back to the section on *The Oldest Profession.*

...frankly, they are all doomed. True love is an impossibility. Lasting relationships? No. Real fulfillment? Never.

I thought of my mother and her whole "string" of men. I thought of my dad, alone. I thought of poor Friday and dear Anna. I thought of Min's six marriages. I thought of the wild, hard-drinking Grandma Pearl. I remembered Grandpa Lefty's ashes in my hair. I thought of Officer Wheedle and his love affair with a motorcycle. I thought of Mitch, alone, lost and hopeless in a jungle war. I thought of donuts, warm and sweet to the tongue and completely devoid of nutrition.

Lasting relationships? No. Real fulfillment? Never.

I thought of the Ems.

I thought of my love.

I felt the thump of my heart and the wind in my lungs, and by the time that little silver paperback hit the surface of the Great Lake Erie, I had turned and headed for Carolina.

twenty-two

Why Is It Like This?

There is never a good phone call at three a.m.

I heard my dad answer. By the time I got to the hallway, Friday had grabbed the phone. He spoke frantically, then made a dash to his room.

"Is it Anna?" I asked, panicked. He was tugging a pair of boots over his half-zipped jeans.

"Seizure. Coma," was all he could say.

"I'll drive you, wait," I said and rushed to find my jeans. Carolina, who had already Shazamed herself dressed, helped me get ready. We were all out the door in about four minutes. I was driving, Friday next to me, Dad and Carolina in the back. It was black out. The headlights knifed the road, which was wound tighter than Friday.

Friday was hyperventilating.

"Hold on, man," I said.

Our car screamed up to the emergency entrance to the hospital, and Friday crashed out of the vehicle without closing the door. My dad was his shadow. Carolina climbed in front with me. I parked the car, and she took my hand as we ran.

Once inside, there was nothing much to do except drink coffee and wait while Friday was in with Anna.

Anna's dad had come home from Alaska by then, and her parents let all of us see her. To say goodbye. My mind was having a hard time coping with that one. How many goodbyes can a person say? Not Anna. Why Anna? Mitch, now Anna. I would say I hurt, but you can't hurt when you are numb.

After we saw her, there was nothing else to do except wait, helpless, for my brother to do what he needed to do. The Lovgrens let him stay by her side. We waited, drinking vending machine coffee from cheap paper cups. We waited, eating bad pastry that was wrapped in cellophane. We waited for my brother so that we could take him home when all was done.

Anna hung on all that day and through the night. She took her final breath, a deep one, just after dawn the next day. Friday never left her side. I couldn't leave Friday. Carolina didn't leave me. Dad watched over us all. I felt helpless and strong, protected and protective, all at the same time.

When Anna did go, Friday wanted to drive directly to the old beach. My dad gave us all hugs then walked home. Carolina took a nap in the sand. Friday and I sat on my rock together. He stared at the horizon for a long time. I remembered when I was last with the Ems and how they just sat there, quiet, until I was ready to say what I needed to say. I became like them.

After a while, Friday got up and started walking up and down the beach, fists punching the air. He found a huge rock, holding it in his hand for a long time, as if thinking about flinging it. But Anna was not a hurt he could just throw away. He dropped the rock in the sand and walked back toward me, head down. He stood at my feet, looking at me.

I thought I knew what pain looked like; I'd seen enough of it. But I never saw it look like that. It was white, without blood. Soft, without bone. Friday dropped to his knees and put his head in my lap. I stroked his thick, brown curls and noticed, for the first time, strands of grey. As he sobbed, my own tears burned my cheeks.

Carolina got up from the sand and walked over to my brother and me. She sat down on the rock, putting her back to mine. I leaned on her.

I felt different that day. About a hundred years older. About a thousand times sadder. And real quiet inside.

The funeral procession for Anna was 300 cars long. The day was clear. There were flowers and tears and little epiphanies as people realized, "oh-my-God-that-could-be-me-or-my-precious-somebody-life-is-too-short-oh-my-God." And just for a moment or two, they held their kids or husbands or wives or lovers closer and thanked their lucky buns they weren't the ones being lowered into that cold hole in the ground.

Grief has kicked boring out of my life, and I'm thinking about rethinking things.

As soon as I stop crying.

twenty-three

What Do You Do?

What do you do when someone dies? When they are dead and buried and all the cold cuts are gone and the casserole dishes are washed and put away? What's next when you look at each other feeling empty and sad? When you keep looking at the door, expecting that person to walk through it? Or hear the phone ring and pick it up, expecting to hear her voice? I'll tell you what's next: a whole lot of empty.

When I lost Anna, I lost my friend and my sister, and my brother, for that matter. The hurt from my own loss was nothing compared to the hurt I felt for my brother. To watch him in pain on top of my own was almost unbearable. My dad closed The Precinct for three days out of respect, but opened it back up after one, because we all needed something to do. We needed to be occupied, and mindless donut making was the perfect something.

After Anna died, Friday didn't sleep. But instead of dragging himself around all tired, he had gotten more and more busy. He was spazzing out, finding things to do, anything, like scrubbing all the clean pots and baking sheets over and over. Or washing and waxing his car. Or alphabetizing his albums.

One day, he walked into The Precinct and said, "The Kreamy Thing is up for grabs."

My dad's ears perked with interest as a, "Why didn't I know about this?" look stomped across his face.

"Why didn't I know about this?" my dad asked. "What'd you hear?"

"Gil Rhodes told me that Old Man Peters came in tossing around dollar figures he thought he could get for the place." Friday climbed up on the donut counter and started pacing. Frantic. Manic. He scared me.

Gil Rhodes and Friday had been the best of friends since they were in rubber pants. Gil's family owned Spanky's, a smalltime convenience grocery/deli. Like us, the Rhodes lived above the store, only there were seven of them, including his mom and dad. Gil was a smack-in-the-middle kid. "A rose between four prickers," he used to say, referring to his four sisters. He also used to

say his life was hell. That was in grade school. I liked the
way he said the word "hell." He made it sound so cool.

Gil and I were romantically linked the summer
before I went into the fourth grade. He was heading for
the seventh. It was all just rumor and innuendo, since the
fact was we were just good friends. He used to pick me
up on his bike after his paper route, then take me to
Spanky's for potato chips and an icy root beer. Those
where the days—sitting under the big old oak outside of
the clapboard-covered store, watching Gil ape his
Cleveland Press customers. The only problem was, Friday
got jealous, so I had to give Gil up.

Nowadays, Gil is in the real estate business. He's
quite a success. He's a funny, friendly guy, and people
give him scoops.

"Ah, Gil told you," Dad said. Watching Friday pace.
He looked concerned.

"Yeah. Dad, let's buy it." Friday's eyes were red. He
looked somewhat tattered and desperate.

"You want to buy The Kreamy Thing?" my dad
asked.

"Yeah, let's do it. You know. It'll be big. It'd be great,
we'll corner the...uh corner," Friday reasoned.

My dad hesitated. "I'm not sure we should be talking
about this right now, son."

"Hey," Friday said, "I only know a ballpark, but I
could do it. Anna and I—" He took a big sob of air.

My dad looked devastated. I started crying.

Friday caught himself, and kept on pacing back and forth on top of the counter. He managed to not knock over even one sugar dispenser. "We. Were. Going to. Buy. A. House. I. Have. Money." Somehow, he controlled that flood of grief inside of him.

"Well, son, why don't we talk about it later?"

"Now!" screamed Friday. "Now! It's my money, I am buying it. I don't want a house. I don't want a house. Not without her. No. No. I'm going to buy it. I'm going to buy it."

"Okay, okay," my dad said. "We'll talk to Rhodes, and I will partner with you."

"Me, too," I said.

The two of them looked at me, silent.

"I have money."

We all have money. Low overhead. Not big consumers. Hard workers. It was a family thing.

Friday looked at my dad.

"If the price is right," I said. If Friday wanted this, or if this was his way of getting through the darkness, I was going to be right beside him.

My dad and I did not want to talk about this. It didn't seem right. I kept looking at my brother. He sat down on the counter, legs swinging.

"Come on. We're doing this. We're family. Forever," said Friday.

"Huh." My dad, I could tell, was trying to figure out the best way to handle the situation.

"Ok, let's look at the business. Maybe it's time for both of you to buy into The Precinct, and we'll expand to The Kreamy Thing."

"Yeah," I said. "We'll be a tight family business. Donuts and ice cream. We'll do great."

They both looked at me.

"What?" I asked.

Friday shook his head. "I thought you hated the donuts, Toby."

"Yeah," I said, "I thought I did, too." What I didn't say, and didn't know clearly until that moment, was that I loved my brother and father far more than I hated the donuts.

I know Friday was grieving hard, and I was grieving hard. We all missed Anna so much. Sometimes, I'd see her coming through the door of The Precinct and I'd smile and start toward her, only to see it was someone else. The person didn't even have to be blonde, or tall. I guess I just wanted to see her so bad. I could only imagine what was going on inside of my brother. Working harder made sense. As I said, it's what we do. The Kreamy Thing, somehow, made sense.

"Well, let's think on this and talk again in the morning," my dad said. "We'll sleep on it. Bee, you have a good head for numbers, and you're a good worker.

Think about what your girlfriend can bring to the party. I think she's a sharp cookie."

I looked at him, the electrodes in my brain sparking at the way he said "girlfriend."

My dad responded, "If she's going to be part of the family, let's use her God-given talents. Make sure she's around tomorrow."

My heart was thudding.

Later, when we were in bed, Carolina wrapped around me in her usual way, I took the long way into the subject.

"Carolina."

"Yeah?" she asked.

"What do you make of us?" I asked back. She sucked in some here-we-go-again air.

"What are you thinking about, Toby? Let's just cut to it."

I told her about the businesses and what my dad had said.

She was interested. "Your dad is cool."

"I think he's figured us out."

"Yeah?"

"I think. But I wonder why he doesn't say anything."

"I told you, he's cool. The guy would do anything for you. So'd Friday."

"So, what about us?"

"What about us, Toby?"

"You think we're forever?" I asked.

"I'm not the forever kind," she said. "I'm the today kind."

"What's that mean?"

"It means, who knows? Nobody knows. I like it here, I told you that. But sometimes things just get screwed up."

"Yeah, I know," I said. "But...."

"But what?"

"It's getting old."

"Listen, I'm a today kind of person, and today we're us, okay?"

"What about tomorrow?" I asked.

"I just told you," she practically yelled, "I don't know about tomorrow."

"I mean, do you want to come to the meeting about the business?"

"Oh, sorry...yeah," she said.

We were quiet for a while.

I put my "good head for the numbers" mind to work and figured that, if I love Carolina today and she loves me today and every tomorrow is a today, then, in a way, we will love each other forever. Thinking it was a good theory and feeling somewhat confident, I told her just that.

"You just don't quit," she said.

I shrugged.

"Just don't quit," she repeated, putting her head on my shoulder and wrapping her leg more tightly around me. "Sometimes I think you saved my life."

"What?"

"You heard me," she whispered.

"I sometimes think you saved mine," I said.

"Well, maybe we saved each other."

"And together, we'll raise the blood sugar levels of Northeast Ohio," I said.

"Together," she said.

"Forever," I tailed.

"Aw, Jesus," said Carolina, just before she brought me to my knees.

twenty-four

The Runaway

When I walked in, the flat was dark. I hadn't seen Carolina since she left for the Texaco that morning. I missed her and was hoping to find her. The TV wasn't on. Dinner wasn't cooking. She wasn't napping. I sat down and opened the latest issue of *Hollywood Stars* magazine I'd just picked up at the drug store. This issue featured John Travolta. Again. The boy was hot with the press. I was hardly past the headline when I heard low voices coming from my dad's bedroom. I was curious—okay, nosey—and tiptoed over to his door. It was open a crack, and as I nosied in, I saw him holding Carolina warmly to his chest. He gently kissed her forehead. I gasped. I saw both sets of eyes fall on me before I ran to the back steps.

I ran. I ran and my head was black. My sight was gone. I ran, blinded by idiocy, to the old beach. I ran on the old beach. Down the old beach. I ran for what seemed miles and miles and miles. Across private property. Through shallow water. I'm not sure what I saw or what I thought I saw in that room, but it scared the brain right out of my head. I finally tripped and fell crying to the sand. I grabbed the sand in my hand, squeezing it until it disappeared over and over again.

When did they connect, and how? My own question kept pushing to my brain. *When did they connect, and how? When? How?*

What had I seen? The two in his bedroom. His arms around her. Her head buried in his chest. A kiss. What was the look on her face when she turned to look at me? I tried to reconstruct it in my head. Passion? Passion. Was it passion? There were tears. There was surprise. Of course, she was surprised. She wasn't expecting me. Why wasn't she expecting me? I'm always home at that time. What was his face? Lust? How would I know what lust looks like on my dad? He was rocking her a little. Concern? Dadness? Dadness.

I sat up, still reconstructing, and the more I reconstructed, the stupider I felt. What was I thinking? My lover and my father were lovers? What the…? Am I so pitifully afraid that Carolina is going to leave me that

I let myself believe that? The idiot I was became clear to me, and I felt all the idiot I was.

What is an idiot to do? Never go back. I sat on the sand, wishing I had brought my coat. Wishing that wishing would make me warm. I started walking to get warm. I started walking back to the Precinct. Embarrassed. Tired. Trying to build the story that would explain my behavior. I remembered I left the BUNN-O-Matic on? I forgot to mail an important letter. I felt a sudden urge to become physically fit? I wished I was a better liar.

I arrived back about an hour or so after my swift exit. I was relieved that nobody was there. I went in to take a shower to warm up. My poor idiot face was covered with sand, streaked with tears. I tried to wash the whole stupid experience away. But while doing so, wondering, *What's wrong with me?*

I was washing and crying when the door opened and closed.

The shower curtain opened, and there stood Carolina, cheeks all blushed from the outdoors. My body blushed pink from hot water and embarrassment. Soap bubbles covered my steaming skin. She stood staring at me with dripping eyes.

"I called my mom today, Toby," she said, tears rolling in perfect little BBs down her cheeks.

"Your dad helped me…. He's been helping me. He's very kind, your dad. Very understanding."

She sat on the closed toilet seat and rested her face on her hands. I was naked and soapy. I got out of the shower without rinsing or drying and crouched down beside her.

"Why didn't you tell me?"

"For some reason, your dad was the only one I could talk to about it. I guess he's the only one I thought could help." She looked at my soapy face, which was becoming dry, caked, and uncomfortable. I was beginning to taste the soap. "I'm sorry," she added.

"It's okay," I said. "What did she say, your mom?"

"Not much. She just started crying. Frank wasn't home."

I hadn't heard much about a mother, much less a Frank. I had a lot to learn, and I decided I didn't want to learn it caked and naked.

"Let me rinse off," I said. "Will you take a walk with me?"

She nodded.

I rinsed, toweled, and dressed. When I came out of the bedroom, Carolina and my dad were having coffee in the kitchen. My dad looked at me, kind of sober. Somber. Hurt?

"Are you ready?" I looked at Carolina.

"Bee," my dad said. "What is it that you thought?"

I looked at him, knowing he knew where my mind had gone. And my mind had gone.

"Nothing," was all I could say. Nothing. "I…I had to go think, I guess."

"So you did some thinking?" he asked.

"Yeah." I nodded.

"Good," he said. "Thinking is good."

I wanted to get out of there at that moment more than I wanted anything in my life, but Carolina sat as if she had sandbags for butt cheeks.

Okay, so they were going to make this difficult. I walked to the cupboard for a cup, all stiff and awkward like I was made of cardboard, and poured myself some coffee. To buy time, I stirred some cream into the dark coffee. I stirred until the cream became the coffee and the coffee became the cream. I tried not to stir much myself, maybe thinking I could become invisible.

Raising the cup to my lips, I finally looked at my dad.

God, why didn't he yell or something? He sat silent. Damn the silent.

"I was scared, Dad. I was insane. How was I to know?"

"I'm your father, Bee. I think you know a little bit about me."

He was right, of course. He'd been steady. Boring, but steady. Weird, but steady. Quiet, but steady. I was beginning to see that he was hurt by what he thought I thought. Which I did think, but hadn't yet confirmed out loud.

"It was only for a minute or two.... I thought...you were in each other's arms.... I didn't know you guys even talked. I felt...hurt, maybe, jealous, maybe." I flinched at my own words.

"But what about me, Toby?" Carolina asked.

I just looked at Carolina. What about her? There was so much I didn't know, it became clear that I didn't trust her completely. Or she me. I loved her, but she was like the weather. I never knew what the day would bring.

"I don't know," I said.

"You don't?"

Lord. "Listen," I said, "I feel like I'm on trial here for something I thought."

"You are." I'm not sure who said that.

"You should have stayed and found out before running away like a child. You're a grown woman now, Bee. It was hurtful, what you did," my dad said.

"I'm sorry. But...." I looked at them, realizing that no "but" would do. "I'm just sorry."

My dad said, "Good. Accepted. Next time, think first, run second."

Then we talked. And talked. My dad had been concerned about Carolina since day one. He started nosing in, asking her questions right away. She didn't answer much at first, but he kept at it. At one point they just started talking. I still don't know when, exactly, but they found time. He eventually got her whole story, which included when and why she ran away.

Ran away.

My girlfriend was a runaway. A runaway teen. Just like on television and in the newspapers. Once again, she became so glamorous to me. My weakness, I guess. But just up and running, just going away was sometimes so appealing to me.

Maybe me running from them was my mini-version of it. It's kind of fun, not thinking. Not talking. Just running with my emotions. Tripping in the sand, tears streaming. It has its appeal. Idiocy and all.

But my Carolina, she did it for real. On a grand scale. The way I had always wanted to.

Seems like Carolina had an okay life early on. At least she remembers having a mom and a dad. Then things changed.

"I remember being happy until...I don't know exactly when. I was in school, maybe first grade. That's when my dad hung himself."

Oh my God.

"My mom wasn't so good at handling that. Or anything, really. She was drunk pretty much all the time. There was nowhere to go and no one to help me. Living with her family, geezus. She had this one brother who was always trying to put his hands all over me. My grandmother was mean as hell. She liked to make me her slave. The other uncle was another kind of creep. My grandfather was a nasty drunk. My mom would disappear for days at a time. Weeks, maybe. Just leaving me with these people. I learned to stay away.

"In the seventh grade my mom got us our own apartment, she was a cocktail waitress then. She'd work seven 'til two in the morning and leave me alone. She'd bring home the men. She'd drink until she passed out. The creeps didn't always pass out. The things they tried to do…. Somewhere in there I took that razor to my wrist. The guy that she had the hots for at the time bailed, and I think she was madder at me for chasing him away than she was about me trying to do myself in. I was put into a mental ward for a while."

She looked so forlorn. I couldn't think of anything to say.

I pulled my chair close to Carolina's and put my arms around her. I kissed her hair. I looked over her head to my dad, who stood wet-eyed. I realized that he knew all. He knew what we were. And he stood there with his heart in his eyes. I loved my dad at that moment. More than I'd ever realized I could.

"She eventually found a steady boyfriend, Frank. I hated Frank. He drank, and he was mean. But he didn't hit me, and he didn't try to touch me. He had a house, so we had a steady place to stay. But he was still nasty to me. And they both drank themselves numb so often, I knew they didn't give a damn about me, so when I got the chance, I took off for New York."

"By yourself?" The thought was unfathomable.

She looked at me. "No, I had a girlfriend. She was five years older. She wanted me to go and asked me why I'd stick around those two. I thought she knew it all."

I immediately felt that jealous thing, but I understood.

"Oh. Did you ever go back?" I asked.

"I called a few times, but that damn Frank always answered, so I'd hang up. I kept calling, trying to hear my mom's voice."

I understood that one. I'd wanted to hear my mom's voice my whole life.

. . . . .

Carolina talked to her mom a lot over the next few weeks.

"Okay, Mom, I'll come see you."

My I'm-going-to-lose feeling started creeping in. It wasn't easy, but I wanted to help her see her mom.

Carolina asked my dad and me to go with her.

"Sure you want me to?" my dad asked.

"Please, Mr. Renfrew, will you?"

I don't think the lure of a sixty-pound trout would have kept him from going.

twenty-five

Turnpike

I wondered how it was that my dad allowed Carolina to move in. I wondered if he knew what we were about right from the beginning, so I asked him during those few days of baring all, when emotions ran high and poured like hot coffee. A time when everyone seemed vulnerable and I thought I might as well join in.

A couple days before we got on that freeway to Detroit, I asked, "So, dad, um, you know about, um, well, Carolina and I, um me, um, huh?"

He looked at me from in front of his fritter dough. From behind his half-glasses, which he wore as if he needed to read the fritter dough. As I stood there watching him, I realized he *was* reading the fritter dough.

He studied it as he worked it. He was beginning to become amazing to me.

Autumn was sneaking up, and he was whipping up a batch of fresh cinnamon-apple fritters. These were very good things. Deep fried, crisp and light. Not too sweet. Fragrant. The smell was filling; there was almost no need to eat them. They even outdid the pumpkin donuts, which were soon to follow season.

"What about Carolina and you, Bee?" He broke through my frittering mind.

I saw at once that he wasn't going to make it easy for me. I'd lied, basically, and he was going to make me walk the lie. I hesitated, thinking I'd just say, "never mind" and move on. But the truth was, the untruth was weighing on my soul. I took a deep breath.

"Dad, you know."

He peered down at me over his tortoiseshells. "Know what?"

"Okay, okay," I started again. "That...that she's my—my girlfriend."

My-my heart was tap-dancing, but I was hanging in.

"My, my," he said, walking to the sink to rinse his hands. He took forever. Washing, then drying them on his apron. No one was in the kitchen but me, Dad, and the fritters-to-be. He picked up his mug of coffee and leaned against the sink, looking me in the eyes. I looked bravely back, trembling inside, but determined to come clean…since he knew anyway.

"When did you know?" I wanted to know.

He took a drink of coffee. "Well, not when I suggested she share your room with you."

I didn't say anything.

"A while after that. When I saw the two of you look at each other. When I heard you arguing, I knew. Then I didn't know what I was going to do about the both of you, so I asked for advice. And when I asked for advice, I realized that everyone else had already seen what took me so long to see. I felt foolish, and I've got to tell you Bee, disappointed in you."

Tears leapt, wetting my lashes.

"Not that you have a girlfriend instead of a boy— that took a little getting used to, but I held you minutes after you were born. I watched you develop. I know Emily and Emaline. I was disappointed because—"

"I know dad, I lied."

He smiled sadly. "That you did, Bee. That you did."

"I'm sorry, Dad."

"Me too. I'm sorry you lied, too. But then I thought, well, maybe you needed this girl. You always seemed so lonely." The L-word sliced me.

"I really gave it thought. I got to know the girl. Carolina. And I liked her, and I thought I'd do more damage. Who knows where she would go? And the way you were acting, I knew you'd follow. Who knows what would have become of you? I thought I could keep an eye on both of you better if you just stayed put. So, I let things be."

Tears dripped, wetting my lips.

"Thanks," was all I could say.

My lips trembled. I closed my eyes. I felt his arms close around me as I sobbed into his chest. He smelled of apples and nutmeg.

"What am I going to do with you, Bee? What am I going to do with you?"

I didn't know, but I thought he was doing just fine.

During this time, I also wrote a letter to my missing mother. There was nowhere to send it. But I wrote it anyway.

~~Dear mother,~~

~~TO: The former Mrs. Renfrew,~~

~~RE: The daughter you left and never looked back~~

~~Dearest Deserter,~~

~~To Occupant~~

~~To Whom it May Concern, (Oh, wait, you're not concerned.)~~

Laura,

My name is Toby. You might remember me. I was the girl child you gave birth to back in 1960. I have a brother, too. Or, as it turns out, a half-brother. The half doesn't count, though, because he's a full-blooded brother to me. And your husband, the guy you married for some reason, he's my dad. Whoever the real guy is doesn't matter. These guys are my family.

I just want you to know that we're fine. All of us. We did okay without you. Just in case you were worried. (Hah!)

I'm over it all now, but I've got to tell you, it wasn't that easy growing up without a mother. Stick a guy with having to tell his daughter about her period. Good one. And Mother's Day? Always a blast. Fortunately, I had Min and Auntie Flo. And the Ems. You remember them? Oh, they remember you. They just didn't talk about you for forever. But they remember you.

I'm grown up now, with a girlfriend. Yeah, I'm a LESBIAN. She is going to see her mother very soon after a long time not seeing her. That made me think of you. Her mom was drunk all the time, but my girlfriend still kind of loves her. I don't remember you, so it's kind of hard to kind of love you. It's not easy to be mad at you either. It's like being mad at the air. There's just nothing there. Not even a place to land a punch.

So, thanks. Thanks a lot for everything. Really. Life's just great without you.

Genetically yours,

Toby Renfrew

When Carolina decided she was ready, the three of us scrunched into my dad's pickup and began winding our way through the smokestacks of Cleveland, headed for the Ohio Turnpike. The only time my dad put miles on his truck was when he drove twice yearly to Florida to fish. Otherwise, he maybe put on ten miles a week. He was a walker. A walker, a fisher, and a donut maker. And a dad. I realized more and more what a dad he was. A dad to all.

All was quiet in the cab, up and across the turnpike, except for the hillbilly music on the radio. Old Hank and Patsy. It was fitting; their heartache matched mine. Only, mine sprang from the *idea* of a love lost, not the actual thing. The cold rain on the windshield didn't stray from the lonesome theme. The splash of traffic and the high, shrieking rhythm of the wipers lent to the mood.

I was tired. Carolina was tense. I thought she looked beautiful even as she chewed her left cheek. I was in love from my newly trimmed toenails to my freshly Prelled hair. And I was nervous. I touched Carolina's hand and she jumped. Then she looked at me and smiled that Carolina smile. I felt hot. My dad leaned forward and put on the defroster.

There are three stops on the Turnpike between Cleveland and Toledo, and an hour between Toledo and Detroit. Carolina's mother lived just outside of Detroit. When we pulled up in front of a kind of dumpy little house, Carolina grabbed my hand. She bit her lip.

"Come up with me?"

Carolina the Cool. Carolina the Worldly. Carolina Who Knew All had become Carolina the Vulnerable, just as Toby the Blind was beginning to see.

Carolina's mother was still in her thirties, but she looked older than my dad. Her hair was dyed a black black. Her skin was pale white and overly wrinkled, like cotton. Her eyes were blue like Carolina's. But they were drowning. She took Carolina in her arms, and there was a cry-fest. She stood brushing Carolina's hair with her hand as Carolina made the introductions.

I felt uncomfortable. When we were invited into the house, I found an excuse not to join them right away. I walked to the back and leaned myself against the house, holding my belly in my arms. It was too much for me. I was jealous of the woman. I was jealous of Carolina. It didn't look ideal, but there was a mother/daughter reunion—the thing, I realized, I'd been longing for my whole life long. But it wasn't my mother/daughter reunion. (Dear Mrs. Renfrew, thanks for nothing.) As a matter of fact, I felt as if this was a reunion that would cut me out of the picture. I felt hurt and cheated and I wanted to run, but those Judas knees of mine could only buckle, and I slid down the side of the house.

My dad came around the corner and found the heap that was me. He crouched down and took my hands in his. His eyes understood. "Oh, Dad," was all I could say as I once again buried myself in him. Damn.

Carolina's mother, Marie, made us instant coffee and served store-bought cherry-chip cupcakes. I sipped sullenly at my coffee while Carolina and her mother searched for words and conversation. I was getting more and more restless as Marie started asking questions.

"So, how did you meet these people, Carolina?"

"Over a cream-filled and some coffee," my girl answered.

"Jelly-filled," I said, not bothering to force a smile.

"Yeah, she just showed up at the donut shop one day, and we decided she was a keeper," my dad said with a great warm grin.

Marie smiled back in a way I'm not sure I liked.

I wanted to get out of there, but I took a cupcake and became busy with the wrapper and my mental critique of its contents. Dry. Fake chips. Bad icing. I ate it anyway. The conversation blurred in my ears. As I started my third cupcake, I felt a hand on my shoulder; it was Carolina's.

"Let's go see what they did to the room I used to have," she said. "Come on."

I followed her down a short hallway to a room that held a single bed covered with a chartreuse and pink bedspread, barely visible under all the junk piled on top. The room looked like a storage locker.

"This never was much of a room," Carolina said sadly. "You know I never really had a room?"

I wanted to be supportive, but I didn't have an ounce of anything to give her at that moment.

She threw a bunch of stuff on the floor, then lay down on the bed in the fetal position. I thought of the word "fetal." I thought "femme fetal." Then I didn't feel like doing any mental word gymnastics. My brain was tired. I looked at my girlfriend. She was sad.

"Not much left of me here," she said. "Not that there ever was much of me here."

I sucked it up and lay down next to my femme fetal to spoon her. We lay there quietly with our own thoughts until her mother came in. Marie stood at the door and announced that Frank was home. I would have gotten up and pretended that I wasn't Carolina's lover, but I was too weary. It didn't matter anyway. Carolina had had a girlfriend before she left home, the "older woman" I'd just learned about. The two of them ran off to New York City to live the big life. They eventually hooked up with a women's motorcycle club and camped upstate until winter. They spent some time in Florida until Carolina's girlfriend fell for someone else. Carolina then traveled with an even older biker to Pennsylvania. The woman, she said, drove her crazy, so she hitchhiked as far as the old beach and into my life.

Few words passed between the three of us. Marie's face was tense. She said again, "Frank's home, Carolina."

Carolina stiffened. "Give me a minute, Mom."

"Mom" echoed in my ears, and I hated Carolina at that second. I looked at the cotton Marie as she spoke. "I don't want to upset him, Carolina. Don't be long, now. I've got dinner on."

Frank was awkward and uneasy. He wore a mechanic's uniform, and I could tell he'd tried hard to scrub grease and oil off his hands. He didn't smile when he saw Carolina.

"You're in one piece," was all he said.

Don't get too emotional, Frank.

We had an awkward dinner. The two men didn't have much to say to each other. Dinner was meatloaf, canned corn, potato buds, and Franco-American brown gravy. I didn't eat much. I just wanted to go home and go to bed. The house was tiny, so my dad got us rooms at the Holiday Inn. Carolina's mother didn't insist that we stay.

We went back to visit again the next day, and we were going to leave right after. That's when Carolina broke the news, saying that she needed to stay for a while.

"With Frank here?" I asked.

"I can handle him now," she said.

"But, why?" I almost pleaded. I knew I was going to be cut out. I just knew it.

"I know you're worried, Toby. Don't be. This really is something I need to do. You can't just run away from family. It's not that clean."

I wished someone had told my mother that.

"Let me stay with you," I said. I did not like the looks of that Frank. And a sneeze could blow that Marie away—or was that just wishful thinking? It was not safe there.

But she did it. My brave girl did it. Carolina stayed in Detroit alone. As in, by herself. As in, without me.

And my dad drove us back to stinky, eerie Dishrag City. Sitting there on the seat next to him, I felt alone. And as hollow as an empty Crisco can.

twenty-six

Living Backwards

I don't know, maybe I just don't get it. Maybe I just live my life all cockeyed and backwards. I was five before I knew we all grew up instead of down. (Although it took me a few more years to believe it.) I thought that you started out life big (old) and got smaller and smaller every year until you just disappeared.

The reason I believed this was that I remembered being twenty and wearing a red dress. Maybe something horrible happened to me in that red dress, because I hate wearing dresses. I've worn few dresses in my life, and have little intention of changing that aspect of myself, but that's how I remembered me when I was five. I remember telling my dad, "Next year, when I'm smaller, I can get a baby cone." I saw a baby eating a baby cone at The Kreamy Thing, and I guess I wanted to be that baby. My dad laughed and corrected me. "No Bee, you're going to be a bigger girl next year."

I remember insisting that I was right and, of course, crying because he didn't get it. What irritates me was that I recently mentioned the incident to my dad and he didn't remember it.

"How could you not remember something so important?" I asked.

"It was all important, Bee," he said.

But anyway, besides that growing backwards thing, except for words and numbers, if there is a wrong way to put something physically together, I'll find it. I sewed the entire hem to the outside of my poncho in home ec class.

If I'm absolutely positive that I should turn right, I'd better go left. And buttoning a cardigan, I can count on doing it twice. I was the kid with her shoes on the wrong feet. And I never understood why, when you have a whole box of crayons, you'd ever color anyone's hair brown. I wouldn't bring all this stuff up, but I am a girl who loves a girl. Not just loves a girl, but *loves* a girl. I'm crazy for the girl. I'm not crazy for a guy.

Could I be? I love guys, I just don't *love* guys. The feeling's just not there. It's like they're all my brother.

They're cool and everything. Some are even cute and handsome and all of that. I found myself at The Tavern one night purposely trying to see them differently. You know, I mean, sexually. I even went out of my way, getting dressed up and digging out my fake ID, to go downtown to a disco to try to dance with one to see what it would feel like. That's where I met Bob.

"Hi," said Bob.

"Hi," said me.

"I'm Bob," said Bob.

"I'm Shauna," said me.

"Shauna. That's a sexy name," said Bob.

"Thanks," said me.

"Wanna dance?" asked Bob.

"Sure," answered me.

I found disco dancing rather awkward, even though I was doing my best Saturday Night Fever.

Bob was no John Travolta.

"Wanna beer?" asked Bob.

"Sure," I said. But I was too nervous to drink it.

Bob wanted to slow dance during the fast songs.

They were all fast songs.

I slow danced with Bob during the fast songs.

I let the beer-soaked Bob kiss me. Bob was faster than the fast songs. The bulge hardened in Bob's sans-a-belt polyesters. Bob asked me to his car.

A true romantic.

I told Bob I had to go to the bathroom, and I ducked out when he went to buy us a couple more beers. I found my old Mustang and—after a few wrong turns—made it home.

I laid awake all night, thinking about being backwards.

I thought about Bob's bulge.

I thought about me.

I thought about the way I feel about Carolina.

I stayed in bed all day, thinking about being backwards.

I thought about Bob's kisses.

I thought about Carolina's kisses.

I thought about our first night together. How there was no hesitation on my part. How I wanted everything she had. How I drank her in. How I felt like I was soaring. How I told her my soul felt like it was singing and how she laughed at that. Then how she stopped laughing. And was silent. And whispered into my hair, "My soul sings, too." I thought about how right it felt right from the start.

I sat by the lake all night thinking about being backwards.

Maybe it was the lake large in front of me, or the sky vast above me. Maybe it was the place I occupied against those backdrops. But, somehow, the notion of growing small made a lot of sense.

t w e n t y – s e v e n

Write On

Dear Carolina,

Come back home NOW.

I don't mean to be bossy, but if that's what it takes, I will be.

Toby

Dear "Mother,"

Go screw yourself.

Sincerely not yours,

T. Renfrew

Dear Anna,

I need someone to tell me a joke right now. I need one of your funny stories. Mostly, I need my brother happy again.

Your mom gave me your snowflake sweater.

I sleep with it. Hope you don't mind.

Oh, by the way, Carolina left for a little while, but she'll be back.

Right? Can you tell the future over there wherever you are?

Your sister forever,

Tobe

Dear Mitch,

I was thinking of you today and pictured you in heaven.

Pretty heavy thought, you there in the clouds, cigarette hanging out of your mouth. I started laughing because I thought of you and Grandma Pearl sneaking smokes when you think God's not looking.

I picked up a pack of Carolina's smokes the other day and read the warning. I am thinking of suggesting to the surgeon general that he create a warning about war being hazardous to your health: "Warning: War can kill you and break the hearts of everybody else." Maybe they should bring back the old Indian peace pipe. Can you imagine a bunch of Washington guys sitting around with the Viet Cong, or whoever, and just smoking it out? I think it's a good idea and one case where smoking could save lives. It would be worth a try.

By the way, we're still looking out for the Camaro.

Luv,

Your cuz

AAAAABBBBBCCCCCDDDDDEEEFFFFFGGGGHHHHHHIIIIMISSCARO
LINA

Dear "Mother,"

Aren't you even curious about me?

I used to be curious about you. But I got over it.

Okay, as I type this I can see that it sounds kind of like I'm not over it. But I am, really.

Wait, that sounds even more like I'm not over it, when someone says, "really," they are trying too hard to convince someone else.

Okay, maybe I'm not over it. How does that make you feel? I never got over it. It's bad enough that you just deserted us, but some people get divorced and still see their kids. Man, you must have some heavy problems. My girlfriend's mother is an alcoholic. Is THAT your problem? Or are you on drugs? Maybe you're in jail. At least that would give you an excuse for not coming around.

People say you were a slut. They don't use that word, exactly—they are too kind—but that's what they mean, which makes me feel great. (Sarcasm.) But at least you had the sense to leave us with a guy like my dad. He's kind of boring, but it's worked out pretty good. Same with this town. I hated this town more than I hated anything. It's boring, too. But now I think that it's up to a person not to be boring. I mentioned my girlfriend, her name is Carolina, not that you are interested, but she came around and thought this town was kind of cool. She came from a shitty place, so she liked this one. It's all perspective, from what I'm gathering. She helped me see good things. Which is a good thing, because I wanted to split. But then, I would have been like you, wouldn't I? Well, maybe not exactly, because I would not be a DESERTER. I would at least visit once in a while.

Carolina's gone now. But I hope she will come back. Oh, wait, that sounds like a theme, doesn't it? Oh, wait, it is a theme. Friday would like his fiancée, Anna, to come back, but she can't, because she's dead. We all want Cousin Mitch to come back. (Remember him? Do you care? No.) But he can't because he's dead. Are you dead? Is that why you don't come back? Carolina's not dead, though. She's not. She's coming back. She's not like you.

Well, "mother," it's been a real pleasure. Let's do this again some time, eh?

Toby RENFREW

Okay, I wrote letters to dead people and dead-to-me people. And to my love who will never see the letter. But pounding the typewriter felt good. The paper listens.

twenty-eight

The Deepwater Blues

One day, in what I now call my blues period, I walked over to Auntie Flo's. Nobody was home, so I went in the backdoor, took Mitch's Camaro keys off the key rack, and headed for the garage.

I opened the garage door and saw that Uncle Nick had been up to his tricks and put a brand-new shine on the thing. The top was down. There she sat, gleaming, even in the dim light of that old garage.

I got into the driver's seat and cranked her up. What a sound. That initial turn of the V8 was like a wind instrument. Not an instrument that plays in an orchestra, but its music was distinct and clear. The radio dial, as always, was set on CKLW-AM. I clicked it on.

Fleetwood Mac's "Go Your Own Way" was playing. *Hum*, I thought, *how appropriate*.

I thought about the years that went by on this radio. From Mitch's favorite, Roy Orbison's "Pretty Woman," to Motown, the Beatles. I heard Janis and Jimi, but I didn't know about them until after they died, which was just about the time that Mitch shipped off. The Beatles broke up earlier that year, too, though the radio kept playing them, along with all their solo and new band records. The years and this radio took me from anti-war songs to disco—from Jefferson Airplane to Jefferson Starship.

In the earlier years, I felt that the music was somebody else's. Like it was Mitch's music—the war stuff and the stuff from Woodstock. But eventually, the music became mine. My thoughts and feelings and experiences all seem to have some song attached to them. Like my life has its own movie score. I love music. And that's all thanks to Mitch and the days that turned into the years of starting up that Camaro.

I always kept my promise to Mitch; that's what kept me coming at first. But after a while, it became another rock on the beach for me. A place to go and be and think. I needed this place. It brought me close to Mitch, even after I knew he was dead.

I looked around the Camaro, clean and polished. Uncle Nick must have given the whole thing a going-over, outside and in. I turned up the radio and leaned back the seat. I imagined Carolina beside me and Mitch and Anna and Friday in the backseat. We were flying down the highway, laughing.

I didn't hear Uncle Nick and Auntie Flo pull up in the driveway. I didn't hear anything until the passenger side door opened and Uncle Nick was climbing inside. Auntie Flo walked by, patted my hand, and the thought "scurried" came into my head as she hustled into the house.

"Whoa, Uncle Nick, you kind of scared me," I said.

"Wouldn't want to do that," Uncle Nick said.

"You got her all polished up, she looks great."

"Yeah, Flo and I have discussed it. It's time to let this go."

Tears jumped into my eyes. I was taken totally off-guard.

"Drive me up to the Secretary of State, would you?" he asked. "You know where that is?"

"Uh, yeah," I said.

With a stomach like a stone, I put her into gear and backed her up.

I'd driven her a few times with Uncle Nick aboard. We'd just go drive around by the lake. Never saying much, of course. I'd see Uncle Nick driving through town, too. Never parking, just driving around. It wasn't a car he took on errands. It was just a car he drove, like taking a dog for a walk.

"So, you're really going to sell her?" I asked, still stunned.

"Flo and I think it's time to put her to good use. Mitch was full of life, and he loved this car. It should be part of someone's life again. Someone should enjoy it. It's a big step for your aunt, seeing that she tends to hang on to things."

"She does tend to," I said. "But won't you miss her? The car, I mean...."

"Toby, Flo and I would like you to have it."

A sob gathered in my throat, and I lived the phrase "burst into tears." I became a human sob for a moment. And I heard Uncle Nick's voice say, "Pull in here."

We were by the city hall. I stopped the car and put my head on the steering wheel and sobbed. I don't know why, it just hit me funny. Maybe I thought I didn't deserve it. Maybe it was the kindness and love that came my way. My uncle sat quietly beside me. When I looked up, I saw the tears cutting rivers in his cheeks. I leaned over and put my arms around him. I had a stomach full of butterflies.

"Thank you," I sobbed. "Thank you." Maybe I said it a million times.

We drove to the Secretary of State. He had the title
all ready to transfer, and he had shined it up one last
time—for me.

I eventually dropped him off and drove to The
Precinct. I parked it in the back, next to Friday's very
cool black Mustang, a hardtop. A fastback. The two cars
looked like they belonged together. The Mustang was a
newer model, but Friday bought it used, just like Mitch
had his Camaro. They were both polished and amazing.
Friday and my dad came out of the kitchen door in back.
I could tell they already knew.

"How about a ride?" my dad said.

My dad got in front, Friday in back. I had put the top
up when Uncle Nick and I drove around, but took a
couple minutes to put it back down. Neither one
questioned me, even though it was late October. The air
smelled like the lake and the last of the autumn leaves.
The gravel crunched under the tires as I backed out of
the driveway. My nose became red and cold as I headed
for the scenic route along the lake to find the overlook
where Mitch and I last hung out.

I wanted to complete the circle.

twenty-nine

The Antidote

She had told me she had to stay. Alone. As in, by herself. As in, without me. But I already iterated that. She said that even though she ran away, she brought everything she ran away from with her. She said she wanted to take all that shit back and leave it where it belonged. She said she had things to work out in her head. Things to work out with her mom. She had things. I tried to understand. I guess I did, on one level; only, I wasn't on that level too often. Mostly, I was in the basement. My heart dropped from its place and was sitting in the sole of my left foot. I couldn't take a step without feeling the swollen organ squishing between my toes.

Life without her was the saddest thing I could imagine. Time was a slug drunk on beer. I couldn't recall my life before her. I was wrecked. Friday and I both faded like ghosts. My poor dad was beside himself. He'd try to buck us up with talk of The Kreamy Thing and buying into The Precinct. Friday's original enthusiasm disappeared. If he had been using the business to ease his pain, he was sorely reminded of his own by mine. I felt guilty and tried to fake it. Then he tried to fake it. All the faking seemed worse than the grief.

We were working in the Donut Shop of Love Lost, serving hollow jelly donuts, deflated cream puffs, éclairs with nothing to declare. These were dark days in the history of The Precinct Donut Emporium. My mind ran with thoughts of my father's forlorn love life, and I began to believe that the shop was doomed from the start, beginning with his deserted heart. Perhaps it was our fate to have no love here. Kasper was single. Min couldn't stay married. Even the conversations of our customers, so many bits and pieces picked up, crumbs of love left on dirty dishes. Maybe The Precinct was a magnet for the lovelorn. A vortex that sucked happiness from innocent, loving souls. I took myself to the bottom of empty. Then I wondered if a vortex sucked and thought I'd look it up.

Later.

Min tried to comfort me.

"It hurts every time, honey, but you'll bounce back," she said as if Carolina weren't coming back. Some comfort.

Your boobs are the only things that'll bounce back around here, I thought. I had no intention of collecting lovers, like *someone* I knew. Okay, I was feeling mean and bitter.

Auntie Flo tried to fix me up with a boy. "Now you should just put that awful phase behind you," she said.

Not a phase.

The Ems hugged me. "Be patient," was all they said.

Patient? I am not patient. I wanted my Carolina and I wanted her now. NOW. This was a problem for me. I was about out of my skin. My grief seemed bigger than me. My body was too small to contain it. I was not doing well. I didn't know what was worse—having your love leave the world (see also, Anna), or knowing that your love was alive and breathing and not being able to touch her.

Why didn't she call? Why didn't she write? It had been weeks. She just stayed there in Detroit, doing Lord knows what, and I was stuck far away in the Land of Cleves. No Loves Land. Then it hit me: I was becoming my father. I didn't want to live life as he had. I ached for my lover.

I was in bed, *alone.* Next to her space. Next to her pillow. I was going to Carolina in my mind when I thought of Friday. He couldn't retrieve his Anna, but I could drive to Detroit. I had the ride.

I grabbed my jean jacket and, in my t-shirt and flannel pajama bottoms, walked from my bed to the Camaro. I turned on the radio and gunned through Cleveland and up the turnpike, then buzzed through Toledo and finally, after six cups of coffee and thirty wrong turns, I was in front of her house.

It was four a.m.

The radio was playing "Yummy, Yummy, Yummy" by the Ohio Express. I turned it off, but it kept playing in my head, driving me crazy. I turned it back on and it was playing "Simple Simon Says." Jesus, where'd all the real music go? I wasn't going to put those songs on my life's movie score.

I got out of the car. I couldn't go knocking on the door, so I went looking for pebbles to throw at her window, like I saw people do in movies. Do you know how hard it is to find pebbles on paved streets at night? Not easy. I wondered if cigarette butts would work. I considered throwing my coffee cups. I tapped lightly on her window. Nothing. I went back to Mitch's...*my* Camaro, frustrated. I started crying. I didn't have any Kleenex. I was cold. I should have planned this better. Suddenly, someone grabbed the passenger door handle and yanked the door open.

I screamed.

"Baby?"

It was her.

There she was in her t-shirt and underwear, long white legs tapering into slim soft ankles joined to bare, red-toenailed feet. She had her blue jeans and a sweatshirt under her arm.

She climbed into the front bucket, grabbed me, and started kissing me Carolina-style. The steam thickened on the window. The car rocked on shocks.

She looked at me through those clear blue eyes and smiled, happy mixed with sad.

"You came to get me," she said.

"I had to, Carolina."

"The car?"

"It's mine now," I said.

"Wow, your family…." She paused. "I'm glad you came. It was time. I did the grownup thing and came back to face them. Your dad thought it would be a good thing for me. He said I could stop running then."

"My dad said that?"

"Yeah. He said he knows what it's like from the other side. But he guesses that it's hard for the runaway, too."

I wondered if that meant he felt some sympathy for my mother. That was a new thought.

"I did my part. I came home and I'm glad I did. Toby, I was the grownup these past weeks. They are still a couple of mean, messed up drunks. Can we get some coffee?"

Oh, boy, more coffee.

We went to a nearby twenty-four-hour donut shop. Twenty-four-hour donuts. I hope my dad doesn't get wind of that one. I had a cake donut with chocolate icing. The cake was good, though not as fresh as ours. The icing seemed canned.

"When I was a kid," Carolina said, "I thought if my mom really loved me, she'd stop drinking."

I listened.

"I don't know if alcohol has power over her, or if she just wants it to take over, but the whole thing's selfish, if you ask me. It's all about her and her booze."

"Did you guys talk at all?"

"Yeah, but she always seemed distracted. And once she started drinking, she'd turn on me. Or worse, it was a sob-fest. I couldn't stand it. It was like I was a kid all over again.

"It's weird. They both get up and go to their crummy jobs, but it's like they can't wait to get a drink when they walk through the door. It was bad when I was a kid. Now it's sad.

"I do think my mom loves me, in her own weird way. I do. But she's got a problem. A very big problem, and it's not my problem. I want to live my life, Toby. *My life*."

I felt myself getting nervous. What did she mean? What did *"my"* mean? I felt myself spiraling down into I'm-going-to-lose-her, but I picked myself up. *No more!* I thought. *No more am I going to pull that bullshit on myself.*

"If you want to live your life with me, at least for now, no strings attached, of course, I'd be open to it," I said. My heart was pounding.

"*Open* to it?" she laughed. Then she looked at me and stopped laughing. She took a deep breath. "Well, if you're open, I'm open."

It was after eight when we went back to her mom's house to get her few things. Her mom came into the kitchen in a rumpled flannel nightgown. She still had mascara on from the night before. Carolina made her a cup of instant coffee.

She hugged her mom goodbye.

"You have our phone number, Mom. Call, okay?"

"Or come visit," I added

Her mom's mouth became a little tight line. She looked at me, and it was not a look of love. I smiled anyway. Carolina, after all, was coming with me.

We were out of there. I pointed my Camaro toward Cleveland. My heart was bursting again. Now it was my love that was bigger than my body. My love was leaking out of my eyes on the drive home.

"Why you crying?" Carolina asked.

My mind was searching for the right thing to say. "I have been driving all night…" I started, but stopped myself. No. I pulled over to the side of the road and threw the Camaro into park. It was time to say it all. Lay it out there. I was going to say what I wanted for my life, screw the risk.

"I don't want to live my life without you. I want you, Carolina. I know that it's a pain in your ass when I say that, but it's true. I know I'm young, we're young, and, well, yeah, sure we've got our whole life ahead of us and there are plenty of fish in the sea and all that crap that people tell me, but it's you I caught, and, I love you, I just know I do. And I don't want to be without you again. I want a life with you."

She reached over and put two fingers on my lips.

My eyes were watering. She put her mouth where her fingers were and bit my lower lip before kissing me hard and long. She sucked my heart back up to its proper place.

"I love you, too," she said, again. "I want to be with you, too. I'm willing to try it—the forever thing you are forever talking about."

I loved that she played with words.

"I want a home. And you're home to me, Toby. You're the white picket fence that holds me in."

"Did you make that up?" I asked. It was corny, but I liked it.

"It was kind of corny, huh?" she said.

With that answer, I smiled. I felt like I'd been on a long, hard journey and all I could think of was going to bed for a long, long time. Not alone.

thirty

The Big Donut

I had called my dad from the twenty-four-hour donut place after Carolina said she'd come back, so they were expecting us—but we weren't expecting them.

We walked in the backdoor and started up the stairs when we heard a whistle. It was Friday.

"Toby," he called. "In here."

Carolina and I walked into the shop, and there they were. All of them. Friday and my dad. Kasper and Min. Uncle Nick and Auntie Flo, who I know came in spite of her core belief that I was going to hell. They had even called the Ems, who stood broad and smiling and hellbound themselves.

They were all gathered around a table that held a cake. Fresh made—teamwork, no doubt. A big, double-layered square cake with a hole in the middle. An oversized square donut. Across the top, written in amazing pink icing were three simple, beautiful words:

Welcome Home Carolina.

I looked at Carolina and saw tears leaking out of her eyes. My nose felt stuffy, and when I saw her tears, mine came pouring out. Everybody in my life was standing there in an oily blur, all the love in the world stuffed into one tiny donut shop located where earth stopped and dove into the lake.

My brain started filming the scene in Zapruder slow-motion. Min cutting the cake and putting a piece on a plate. My dad taking the plate, smiling at Min, then turning to hand the plate to Em, who then passed it to Em, who looked to pass it on to Kasper, who put his hand up and mouthed the words, "You take the cake."

Friday, with plate in hand, taking a bite from his fork, laughing at something Carolina said as she held her cake plate, not taking a bite yet. The silent movie of them all played in my head, the edges of the film a soft vignette.

"Bee." It was my dad, trying to poke a plate into my hand.

I took it and looked at him, at his brown eyes clear and happy in the moment. "Thanks, Dad."

He smiled and turned back to Min with a new smile. Min looked at him softly, sweetly, and my insides said, "Whoa." How did I miss that one? Maybe I was just too busy with myself to see how into each other they were.

I looked at Auntie Flo, who didn't take any cake, standing apart from us. I walked over to her.

"Would you like a piece of cake, Auntie Flo?" I asked, handing her my plate.

"No thank you," she said stiffly.

"Oh, okay," I said. "Um, thanks for coming."

"Well, it doesn't mean I approve," she said.

"I know, Auntie Flo. I know."

"The Bible says…" she began.

I looked at her as her eyes filled with tears.

We stood staring at each other for a moment.

"Oh, who knows what God's thinking?" she said. "Or if he has a plan at all?"

Her face was full of pain. "You live your life while you can," she said to me. "Live it. Live all of it."

"I will, Auntie Flo." I paused for a minute, screwing up my courage, and then said, "You do the same, Auntie Flo. You have a life to live, too. I want you to be a part of mine…of ours. Please." I handed her my cake plate again.

She looked at me, smiled a small smile, took my cake, and looked over at Carolina. "Lord help us all," she said as she took a bite.

Later that night, Carolina and I were walking along the beach. It was cold. While we weren't looking, winter had stolen in and settled. The beach grass was brown and frozen. Beer cans played in the waves by the shore, the remnants of another trespasser. I was never comfortable with other people having an attachment to this place. Or to the woods. Or anything that I considered mine. I had slowly begun to realize that I could not possess anything, really. Not the woods, not the beach, not even Carolina. I needed to enjoy what was offered me while it was there. Spending my time worrying about losing it—anything— guaranteed that I would lose the moment I was in.

I pulled off my glove and reached out for Carolina's hand. I took off her glove and put both of our hands in my pocket. Her hand was warm in mine.

"You're sweet, Toby," she said.

"I love you, Carolina," I answered.

"I love you, Toby," she said.

We walked quietly.

"I never knew I could be this happy," she said.

I squeezed her hand. Who knew six months ago that I could *be* happy? Happy here in this town. Who knew that a skinny girl would blow into our donut shop and know more about me than I knew about myself, when I knew me my whole life?

I looked over and saw Carolina's silhouette, loose hairs blowing in the winter cold, lit by the moon over Erie.

Yeah, who knew?

thirty-one

The Jacket

You know I'm not materialistic. I'm no Auntie Flo. I'm the opposite, really, which is why I had practically every dollar I earned since age five compounding daily in the bank and could easily buy into The Precinct and The Kreamy Thing, which we eventually did decide to do. The way I always figured, there are two things that are finite in life—time and money. If you spend your money on stuff, that's one finite thing that's gone—i.e. the money which you only get so much of. If you've got stuff, you've got to take care of said stuff, and there goes that other precious commodity, time. So, I figure, the less I've got, the more I've got.

That being said, there was this one thing that I had to have. When I was in high school, I wanted this black leather motorcycle jacket I saw at Mandelo's. I talked about it. I was obsessed.

On my fifteenth birthday, I got the jacket. Leather and rivets and fringe, the works. Friday, my dad, Kasper, and Min all chipped in and bought it for me, which was almost more beautiful than the jacket. Almost. It was mine and I wore it around school all day, mostly because I was afraid to leave it in my locker. I put a "T.R." in marker on the tag. I marked it mine, mine, all mine.

Well, there was this girl named Cynthia who came from a desperately poor, tragic family situation. When she was three, the family got into a car crash on the way home from a drive-in movie. Her parents and two of the kids were burned to death, and her surviving brother was thrown through the windshield, cut up, and terribly disfigured. His face was covered with scars, and little tufts of hair stuck out on his head. His name was Frankie, and all the kids called him Frankiestein. Cynthia, who was left at her grandmother's that night, spent her life sticking up for her big brother.

I saw Frankie on my first full day of first grade. I was eating lunch when he sat down across from me. I tried not to look at him, because he made my stomach flop. I remember him working on a peanut butter and grape jelly sandwich, squishing it all up until it looked like a bruise. He stuffed the whole Wonder Bread bruise in his mouth and proceeded to chew it with his mouth open. The bruise sandwich and that purple-scarred skin of his was too much for my nervous little six year-old-self. I ran from the cafeteria crying.

One day, I was minding my own beeswax, eating my hot lunch when he came and sat right smack next to me. I was feeling edgy, watching him from the corner of my eye. I'd hardly begun to eat, so I didn't think I could just leave. Then again, I couldn't eat because I was so nervous, and he always made me lose my appetite. So I was sitting there, frozen in place, when he said, "Hi."

"Hi," I returned, staring directly at my "baked Italian spaghetti."

"My name is Frankie," he said.

"Oh," I said, staring at my "buttered green beans."

"What's your name?" he persisted.

"Toby," I said, stealing a look at him while attempting a smile.

That's when I noticed his grass-green eyes for the first time. They caught mine and I found myself staring deeply into them. He smiled broadly.

"You're prettish," he said.

I felt a funny kind of happy. I'd heard the word "pistol" when grownups spoke of me. And "piss and vinegar." And "tomboy," and the dreaded "solid." But never "prettish" which was almost nearly "pretty."

I think I liked it. "Oh," I said again.

I looked straight at his scarred face. "I like your eyes," I said.

He smiled a big, brand new permanent teeth smile.

Well, Frankie and I became lunchtime friends that year and through the next three that he remained in the school.

Kids teased us, but I didn't care. Frankie was the coolest boy I'd ever met. Gentle and sweet and full of giggles and great ideas. I never saw him after he left grade school. Sometime in the ninth grade, he stole a car and they put him in juvy.

Anyway, years went by to find me in tenth grade geometry class figuring out the angles when I felt two hot eyes on me. The eyes were Cynthia's. I looked at her, puzzled, and she looked the other way. Later, at my locker, Cynthia came up and said hi.

"You were my brother's friend," she said.

"How is he?"

"Not so good," she said, then quickly changed the subject, saying, "I have a jacket just like yours."

"Really? I've never seen you wear it."

"Well, I do."

Three times a week, I had to take the jacket off for gym class. I locked it up real secure. But this one day when I came back to my locker, it was gone.

After that, I saw Cynthia in her jacket, just like mine. Suspiciously so. I had never seen her wear it before mine went missing. I thought she'd set the whole thing up. I was sure of it. For weeks, I was sure of it. Positive I was right. When my rightness turned to righteousness, I marched up to her to demand to see the tag. On the tag, I was sure I would see a "T.R." in marker. But when I got closer, I saw her eyes, grass-green like her brother's. Grass-green and gorgeous, standing out against her perfect soft white skin. A shock shot through my body. I'd never noticed her before, not like this. I felt something funny in my belly. I think I stopped breathing. All I could squeeze out was, "Nice jacket."

She said, "I told you I had one."

I said, "Uh."

"We like the same things, huh?" she said, slowly, intently into my eyes. Then more slowly yet, "I guess we have some things in common." Her eyes were shining. Her brows were a question mark.

I was blushing.

"Where's yours?" she asked.

"My?" My synapses had collapsed.

"Jacket."

"Jacket? My jacket, um, it's gone, uh, I lost it…I guess."

Her face fell. "Oh, that's too bad." She said it with genuine sympathy.

I walked away a little dazed.

She was everywhere after that. Green eyes looking like a summer lawn, white teeth flashing into a smile. I began to get panicked for a reason I did not understand.

One day, I walked into the girl's lav where she stood alone, washing her hands.

"Hi," she said.

"Hi." I tried to brush by, nervous. She stopped me and right there in front of the sink, the row of dirty mirrors and toilet stalls she kissed me. Another shock ran from my lips to my toes, hitting a few other tender places on the way down. I kissed her back.

Just then, a group of girls came in talking, laughing, and lighting cigarettes. Cynthia looked square into my eyes for an eternity, then turned and left. Three days later, I found a jacket hanging in my gym locker with a note: *Sorry you lost your jacket. You can have mine. Cynthia.*

I tried to give it back to her, but she wouldn't take it. I started avoiding her. I was feeling all kinds of uncomfortable feelings. I found myself thinking of her much too often. Especially after she left. I heard her grandma died and she dropped out of school.

I could never wear the jacket. I hung it in the hall closet, and it's been there ever since.

"Wow, whose is this?" Carolina asked, grabbing the jacket, modeling in her t-shirt and long johns. Lord, she was sexy.

"It's mine…I guess…" I mumbled.

"Hey, if you're not sure, maybe it's mine."

"You can have it," I said.

"Hey, thanks, babe," she said. Then saw the Lord-only-knows-what look I had on my face and asked, "What gives?"

I told her the story. She took off the jacket and read the tag.

"No T.R." she said.

"Nope."

"Wow," she said. "She had the hots for you, huh?"

"You think so?" Carolina had voiced what I had suspected. I also suspected the feeling was mutual.

"Can't blame her," she said.

"All I know is I felt awful. I was so suspicious. So righteous. That's why I don't wear it. I wish she would have taken it back."

After a long pause, Carolina said, "You should wear it."

I looked at her, waiting for her off-the-wall reason.

"You'll never get a gift like it again," Carolina said. "That girl gave you everything she had."

She wasn't so off-the-wall.

"Here, put it on for our sister, Cynthia," she said. I put the jacket on for the first time ever. "Sexy."

"Yeah?" I said.

"Yeah."

I nodded, looking in the mirror.

"Come on, let's get dressed," she said. "If it looks that good with jammies, imagine what it will look like with a pair of tight Levis straddling Officer Wheedle's Harley."

"Don't even think of it."

"Already have," she said.

So began another day in my life with Carolina.

Acknowledgments

Many thanks to my editor Lisa Cerasoli, and her team, Adrian Muraro and Danielle Canfield, who took on the tasks of untangling my tenses, creating a beautiful interior design, and escorting me through the interesting process of publishing.

Big love to designer Sarah, my good friend who poured talent and sugar all over this book to create the cover. Thank you to designer and friend Basia, who made the donut icon just right, and to friend Nicholas, for saying, "I want to come over and photograph you." Thus, supplying the back-cover photo.

Many thanks to Kathy and again to Sarah. Both of you encouraged (pushed) me to put this story into print. And to my lovely sisters, Barbara and Suzanne, for your invaluable help.

And to my patient partner, Julia, whose constant understanding of the words, "I've got to write tonight." And, "I have to edit this," enabled me to bring this project to its completion.

Read more at our site:

www.thesquaredonut.com